Five-Minute
Erotica

To Robert,
For erotic times short and long.

Library of Congress Control Number 2003090671

ISBN-13 978-0-7624-1560-1
ISBN-10 0-7624-1560-6

Cover and interior design by Amanda Richmond
Typography: Bembo

This book may be ordered by mail from the publisher.
Please include $1.00 for postage and handling.
But try your bookstore first!

Running Press Book Publishers
2300 Chestnut Street Suite 200
Philadelphia, PA 19103-4371

Visit us on the web!
www.runningpress.com

Five-Minute
Erotica

Carol Queen

RUNNING PRESS
PHILADELPHIA · LONDON

Contents

Introduction

Short erotica. Sweet and spicy little bites of fantasy, sexual reveries to look for your own reflection in. This book is a collection of different visions of the erotic, all short, but with no less depth and power for that—any fancier of miniatures knows how much color and detail can be delicately brushed onto a tiny canvas.

Stories this brief are sometimes called "sudden fiction." It's a form especially suited to erotica. Perhaps you know from experience how fast a sexual fantasy can take hold, transport you for a second (or much longer) out of mundane reality. Or perhaps you need to get out of your head, need a match lit to get your fire started. Got five minutes? Start reading!

These stories aim to appeal to heterosexual women's sense of the erotic, but anyone who has paid one bit of attention knows how diverse female desires can be. This book is as diverse as I could make it, for as an editor I never know for sure what will spark the hottest fantasy, make a reader glow or dream. And that's the idea: to get you dreaming; not only the dreams of the authors collected here, but your own. And if men like this book too—well, why wouldn't they? All this talk of Mars and Venus throws an eclipsing shadow over reality: often we share erotic moments, desires, inspirations quite happily.

Not all of the stories are by women authors; I like it when we talk to each other across society's lines. Sometimes we inspire each other; sometimes we learn something about each other.

From sweet musings about (or by) Mr. Right to randy couplings with Mr. Right Now, this collection takes women's different desires in all directions—mild to wild, from the marital bed out to the streets. Our protagonists make love with their longtime partners or go have sex with strangers; they luxuriate in passionate, worshipful oral sex or they show off brazenly. Many of the commonest women's fantasies are here, but it doesn't matter how many women share them, really—what's important is how they feel to you, whether they open a door into deeper eroticism.

Some stars of the erotic writing world contributed to *Five-Minute Erotica*—if you go back to the bookstore, you will see their names everywhere, from their own collections to the content page of Best American Erotica. (Check Contributor Bios for more from your favorite storytellers.) But there are also first-time writers here, several whose stories have never before been published. Four couples contributed stories, too. There's got to be a message in that: The family that fantasizes together . . . ?

Whether or not you and your love (if you have one, or only one) write salacious tales to each other, by all means read these out loud! The stories are quick, sparkplugs to exploration, but they can take you to a place outside of time. Whether you visit in mind or also in body, I wish you a delicious trip.

—Carol Queen
San Francisco, January 2003

Seduction

By Cecilia Tan

She knows what seduction is, because until the night she lost her virginity—a night she had waited for a long time after many near-misses, several broken dates and a few broken hearts—she had thought what most people think, that seduction is something dishonest and dangerous, sultry and tawdry, slow and cautious, but really it's none of those things, for as she learned, the most important part of a seduction is the removal of fear—that instinctual safeguard without which one feels perfectly secure, safe as a hatchling nested deep in downy feathers, for that is exactly how she felt when he—he who is only significant by the fact that it was he who seduced her, finally, that night in the hotel bar where she sat waiting for someone she didn't know would be him—pulled her hand gently until she was near enough to feel his warmth, and he pressed the backs of her fingertips to his fly as if to show her it was nothing dangerous, the way they let small children touch snakes in a zoo, with a care and deliberation that says it is safe, and it did seem so, it seemed hungry to her, but not in a predatory way, rather more like a pet needing to be cared for, harmless and within human control, and so it was that she was seduced, not slow, but quick and sure, so that the panic, the fear, that had driven her from all the others was entirely absent, and she embraced him like he was a big, dependable dog ready for an afternoon walk, but of course they went straight to his room and stripped out of their clothes, quickly, to keep ahead of the fear in case it should return; that is why she was the one who grabbed him by the shoulders and pressed him down, and pressed herself upon him as she looked into his face flushed with thrill and surprise, engulfing him, because she was not afraid in that moment, and now knowing what she did, would not ever be again.

Dear Marla

By Greta Christina

To: Marla (marlabird@thistlebooks.com)
From: Chris (clv@compufix.com)
Subject: I miss you

Dear Marla,

I miss you. The flight went smoothly and my family is relatively sane, except Fran who's having fits about Mom's birthday being perfect. I guess I didn't help matters by calling her Franny-Fat-Fanny, which after thirty-odd years still makes her yell at me. I'm sorry you couldn't be here to see it.

This is what I'm thinking about you today. I'm remembering something I read once, about how 95% of sex scenes in movies show the couple having sex for the first time. I don't know if they meant that number literally or were making it up to make a point. But I realized that I don't get that. I know all these guys (women too, probably) who get bored doing it with the same person, who need a fresh body every few months or years to keep their attention. But I don't get it. I've never gotten it. It seems so ridiculously obvious to me that sex gets better with time, not worse. It's like playing the piano. You need to practice, for years. You can't play the piano for a few months and then quit and switch to the tuba, and then quit that and play the saxophone for a while. Not if you're going to be really good at it.

When I'm going down on you, for example. (What a nice example.) There's a spot, I don't know how to describe where it is, it's on the right side of your nub, kind of high up at the top. When I'm licking you, if you're tensing up and I can tell you're ready to come but don't want to yet, if I lick that spot you kind of relax and go to this other place, this place that's blissful and peaceful and sort of like an orgasm but not one. All that shark-like forward motion stops, for both of us, and it's like sitting still for a moment in the woods. Until I move, over to one of your serious hot spots, just a millimeter down is all it takes, and you start squirming again.

And those hot spots, for another example. When we were first going out, I'd stumble on one and you'd jump out of your skin, and I'd think, Aha! Money in the bank. And I'd zero in on it and make you crazy for about ten seconds, and then a second later you'd get kind of numb and irritable, and we'd be back to square one. Now I know. It is like money in the bank, but I can't spend it all right away or it'll be gone. I know I need to tease it, court it, circle around it, pass my tongue over it for just a quarter of a second and then move away. I know I need to get you worked up, missing it, wanting it, before I come back to it again, for half a second this time, just a couple of hard flicks with the tip of my tongue before I slip off again. I know I can't zero in on it until you're making your final run. And I know that once I do start zeroing in, once you've got your momentum going, I absolutely can't stop.

I didn't know any of this seven years ago. I didn't know a lot of it four years ago. And if I'd dropped you after six months for someone with different colored hair or a different bra size, I'd never have found out. It's an awful thought. I can't stand thinking about it.

It's not like I know things, so now I can go down on you the right way, the same way, every time. It's like, I know things, so I can mix them up, play with them, shuffle the deck in a different way. I can creep up on a hot spot slow and steady like a glacier, or I can flick at it and flick away and then flick back again, or I can dance around it all night and drive you crazy, make you wonder if I'm ever going to get there. I can run my fingers up and down your lips, or use my fingers to spread you apart and open you up so your clit can't get away, or put one inside you for that sensory overload thing that makes you so twitchy. I can press your thighs apart and hold them there, firmly and just a little roughly, like a manly-but-sensitive hero in a romance novel; or I can stroke them on the inside with the tips of my fingers, a light brushing, almost subliminal, adding a bit of background and complexity to the picture I'm drawing on your pussy with my tongue.

It's always new. Always a different mix. The time we did it at Dinosaur National Park, giggling and trying to stay quiet and bumping into the tent poles. That time we called in sick and spent the day in bed together, ordering take-out and watching videos and having sex all day. The night before my father's funeral. Last night before you drove me to the airport. Every time is different.

And that's just going down on you.

Anyway, it's a moving target. You change, I change. Our bodies, our thoughts, our desires. The minute I think I know you, you come up with some dirty new idea, or remember some dirty old idea that's been in the back of your mind for years and now can't wait another second. And I'm dying of curiosity. I can't wait to find out whatever new thing it is I'm going to learn seven years from now, or three months from now, or a week from now when I get home.

All of which is a long-winded way to say that I love you, and I miss you, and I wish you were here to try all this long-winded theory with in person. I'll write again in a day or two. I'll see you in a week. Keep the hot spots burning.

Love,

Chris

Bad Kitty

By Thomas Roche

She's dressed up for the party when I get home from work. She's lying on the bed, sprawled out on her back with her arms over her head, a smile on her face. Her skintight black leotard has a white panel over the belly. Her legs are bare, black ballet slippers on her feet. Her fingernails, long and sharp, are painted black. Also painted black are the tip of her nose, and her lips, which curve as she smiles at me. Her dark hair is pulled into a ponytail and she's got little black cat ears. I have no idea how she got those long, dark whiskers to stand out so straight, but they look fetching, making her dark-painted mouth look even more kissable than usual.

"Meow," she says, rolling back and forth on the bed. "Mrowrr!"

"Bad kitty," I say, smiling. "You're not supposed to be on the bed! You'll get hair all over it."

"Mrrrooowwwrrr! Meow! Mew!" she sighs, and tips her head to bump it against my arm, rubbing against my skin invitingly.

"Bad, bad kitty. Very bad kitty," I say, coming over to the bed and sitting down next to her. "Bad kitty." I start running my hand over her white belly, stroking her.

"Purrrrrr," she sighs.

"Very bad kitty," I say. The leotard is so tight that it clings to the lips of her sex, and I can see them swelling as I stroke her and she purrs. Her nipples stand out firmly through the leotard, growing harder. I pet lower on her belly, nearing the black part, nearing her sex.

"Mrrrowr!" she snaps, clawing at me playfully, bringing her legs up to drag me further onto the bed. "Grrrrrr!" She digs her teeth into my shoulder and starts clawing my back.

"Bad kitty," I say, and extricate myself from her grasp. She looks up at me looking like she just ate the canary. Then, with slow movements of her lithe limbs, she begins to wash herself.

Her pink, pierced tongue lazes over the inside of her wrist, and I can see she's trying to suppress a smile as she coils herself onto all fours and bends down to lick her thigh. She's amazingly limber, but she still can't manage it with the grace of a cat. The leotard plunges low in the back, revealing her spine and approaching the crack of her butt. I start to caress her bare back.

"Purrrrrrr," she coos, stretching out fully on the bed. She starts pushing her ass in the air as I run the strokes of my hand down her back—just like a real cat. This one has a different effect on me, and I feel my cock stirring as she wriggles her kitty behind back and forth high in the air. I spank her butt hard right at the place where her leotard ends and she yelps and meows, clawing the bedsheets. Then she turns toward me. "Hissssssssss!" she says, and claws at my arm, leaving angry red marks until I go back to stroking her butt gently. She pushes her face into the sheets and moans softly, "Purrrrrrrrr."

I slide my hand down between her parted thighs and press my fingers against her cunt. She utters a confused cat sound, sort of a "Mrrrowr?" and pushes back against me, purring. I tug the crotch of her leotard out of the way and find her cunt extremely wet, her clitoris hard and sensitive as I touch it. She wriggles back and forth, purring as I stroke her back with one hand and her pussy with the other. She looks at me, eyes glazed in that way cats get when you've touched exactly the right spot. I slide two fingers into her and the confused cat noise comes again, followed by a long, rapturous purr as she pushes herself firmly onto me.

Still holding her leotard out of the way, I slide under her, my body hanging half off the bed as I pull her down onto my face. My tongue laps her pussy hungrily like a cat going after cream. Again the "Mrrowr?" and again the purring, as I find her clit and stroke it with my tongue. She purrs louder, settling down on top of me as my tongue burrows between her lips and works on her clit. My arms are around her and I'm stroking her back, bringing more purring. My cock stands hard in my pants. She lifts her ass high in the air, tugging her pussy away from my mouth. When I get out from under her, she looks at me and says perkily, "Mrrowr?"

I take my cock out and snuggle up behind her, pulling her leotard back out of the way. Now she's purring rhythmically, urging me on. I guide my cock to her pussy and enter her with a single thrust, listening to the delighted "Mee-yow!" as my cock slides easily into her juicing pussy. I pump into her slowly, and she reaches down to touch her clit as I fuck her doggy style—or, more accurately, kitty style.

I hear her meows coming faster, louder as I fuck her, as she rubs her clit. When she finally comes, it's in a long, low growl of pleasure, a shrieking wail like the cats mating on the fence outside our bedroom. Then she resolves herself into a long purr as I keep fucking her until I moan in pleasure and come inside her.

When I curl up next to her in the bed, she pushes her head against my chest and starts rubbing it, purring.

I look at her suspiciously, remembering.

"Today's Thursday," I say. "Not Friday."

"Mrrowr?" she asks me.

"The costume party's tomorrow night," I say. "Not tonight."

"Mrrreeeow," she smiles, and starts washing my face with her tongue, making me laugh.

"You're a very, very bad kitty," I tell her. "A very bad kitty."

"Puuuurrrrrr," she says, and licks my nose.

For You

By Robert Morgan

Sit down, baby. That's right, close your eyes and breathe easy. I'll take care of you now. First I'll take off your shoes and rub your feet—like this. Do you like the way I hold you, touching you closely with the warm skin on my big hands? Sliding my palms around your foot's tight arch—I want you to feel me running my long fingers around your foot and lifting your leg up a bit as I slide my hand up your leg to your knee. I'll take off your stockings next—be still. Is it o.k. to feel my hands and arms on your calf as I do this? I hope so, baby. Now turn over and sit up. Here, let me help—hold my arm. I'm unbuttoning your blouse now. Kiss me as we do this. Slowly, very slowly touch your lips to mine as my hands take your soft blouse apart. Feel and taste our sweet breath together—our hearts beating faster, I gently press my lips harder onto yours. My arms surround you as I take you against my strong chest, both of us reaching for something inside. Breaking our kiss we pant together as I unclasp your bra and let it slip down. I pull us together tightly and our flesh connects with breathless abandon. My hands run slowly around you, circling our arms into the embrace of new-met lovers. Passion and a warm candlelit room protect us from the outside world as we form a small place of our own. With gasping regret I break our kiss. Now, smiling, I put my hand between your breasts and push you backward onto the bed. Without my asking you bring your hips up. Reaching to your waist I take your skirt off with one long, strong pull. You are almost naked now, on the bed below me, and I tell you again to be still. I reach behind me and grab my t-shirt, pulling it over my wide shoulders to expose my chest and stomach to you. Dropping my shirt and reaching down, one button at a time I undo my pants, then let them fall. Both of us are nearly naked. I'm kneeling next to you. My eyes meet yours, lovely and welcoming. I reach for you and kiss your cheeks and eyes. Your hands, tentative and gentle, touch my chest and ride down my firm belly past my navel to the edge of my hair. My hands and fingers find yours and I guide your arms over and to either side of your head. Leaning over and sliding my muscular length across you I hold your hands down, that and my weight keeping you pressed to the bed, and place my lips just out of reach of your hungry mouth. We are breathing together, just out of touch, and you moan "Please?" into my mouth. Wanton and pleading is where I want you. Ready. I hush your lips with a newly released finger and sit up on your hips. Again, you reach for me, this time with your hands. I hold your arms and place them gently to either side on top of my strong thighs. "Keep them there, baby." I stroke your face, featherlike, touching your warm skin with fingertips. Glancing down over your cheeks and jaw I see the quick pulse in your neck. Placing my palms down on your shoulders I slowly slide my hands up and over the sides of your breasts. Again I move my hands over you, close, but not yet onto your nipples, then let my palms continue gently lower. Lower, to the same place you put your hand on me. Not going any further than you, I rub deeper and run my now-hot palms up your flanks and sides, up your sides and over your breasts, again not quite touching your sweet nipples. We're breathing together again. Against my need to become frantic and mount you I begin to move even slower. With a dreamlike quality to my touch the tension becomes voluptuous, my hips moving involuntarily. Tightening my hard buns against your soft thighs my hands stretch up and move softly onto your breasts. Feel the heat in my palms as I approach your nipples. Aching with need, ready for my loving hands, you arch into me. Quiet for a moment, skin swells into my touch as your heartbeat throbs into my fingers. Your hand moves and reaches down for me. We are suddenly, deeply together, alone, outside the world. Leaning over, I drop on my side, stretching my thighs out next to yours. Grabbing your shoulder I roll you toward me. Insistent now you pull me against you, throbbing heat in your hands. Reaching behind your head my fingers twine into your hair—I force my soft lips against yours. Your free hand involuntarily pushes at me, trying to push me away, then acquiescing—your arm snakes around my back to pull at my shoulders, opening your thighs just a bit and wedging me between them. Writhing your self against me your breathing quickens, full deep breaths as your insistent hand on me begins to arouse my mindless response. Slippery, our juices begin to mix, as you squeeze me again and against your very center. We are as one body now, unconnected yet gasping in full rut. I rise up and kneel, placing my knees between yours and lean forward to lick the inside of your thighs, moving my wide-mouthed sucking lips and soft tongue higher toward the junction of your thighs and mons. My hand is holding you there now as I slide my tongue in a wet sweep to your labia and open you with my lips and fingers. Sliding a smooth finger into your perfect wetness I'm starting to gently suck your clit up into my mouth while my finger moves slowly, deeply into and then out. . . .

I'll stay right here, my love, my darling, until you tell me to stop.

The Bounty of Summer

By Carol Queen

We stop at farmers' markets whenever we're on the road, especially in July when the peaches come ripe, timed with the Perseid meteor showers. We get enough fruit to sate any summer hunger, not just peaches but whatever is juicy and sweet, bearing it away in brown bags as if we are smuggling jewels.

At the bed and breakfast we get a room overlooking the Pacific—we can see it from our bed and from the huge Jacuzzi in the bathroom. It's the honeymoon suite, though we are not married, just fucking like it's the only thing we will have to do for the rest of our lives. We've come equipped with candles to make the Jacuzzi room a wet cathedral of fuck. We stay in the water all weekend, except when we're in the bed. We get out to pee and refill the water bottle so we don't pass out and drown.

We float one at a time, holding each other's heads. He can reach my pussy too because his arms are so long. He sits on the tile edge while I suck his cock, then we switch places. I brace myself on the edge while he fucks me, and we fuck as often as possible. It doesn't matter if he's hard—we both have fingers and tongues, and a bag of sex toys too if it comes to that.

He tells me to close my eyes: His voice is my blindfold. His hands roam on me everywhere, warm, wet as the water. He has turned on the jets and positioned me over one. Everything about me is open, so open, except my eyes. I can picture him anyway, his hands covering my breasts, sliding down, sliding back up to grasp the back of my neck, pulling me in for a wet and melting kiss. I float in his touch, in our sex, like a lotus on a pond, anchored.

A cold something interrupts the warm. Cold and completely smooth, not icy, but a shocking cool compared to warm water and hot kisses. He runs the thing up and down my body, rolls it, really; it seems round or ovoid. I still do not open my eyes. Over my nipples, the coolness tugging them into even tighter erection. Down my belly, giving me the ripply butterfly feeling I sometimes get when I'm touched there. Between my legs, of course, everything we play with goes between my legs, smooth and chill on my clit, nuzzling my cunt lips apart.

It feels like it wants to enter me, nudging the way his cock does, and rounded like a cockhead; but so much cooler than his cock, a little bigger too perhaps. Pushing in—he's lubed it, whatever it is, it stretches the lips, slides in and in. He makes sure it happens slowly. It is big, I realize, wider than his cock, big enough that I have to fight with myself a little to take it.

Suddenly it slides all the way in—it's passed the midpoint and the slide is unstoppable—I'm filled.

He tells me to open my eyes.

There on the edge of the tub one of our paper bags of fruit sits open, full of gleaming red plums not quite the size of a small fist.

"Do you want another one?" he asks, and holds one up for me to bite, juice running down my chin, down my tits.

Ah, the bounty of summer. We eat more plums while he fucks me, his cock nudging the fruit and barely fitting, juice running everywhere. Laughing.

Captain, May I?

BY ELISE MATTHESEN

$\mathcal{T}$he thing about Jeff, thought Brenda, was that he made a person comfortable about doing things for the first time.

Oh, she'd had lovers already. Well, o.k., two, but that qualified for the plural, right? This wouldn't be the first time she'd had sex. Just the first time she'd ever talked about it. Before Jeff, talking about sex had been, "Do you want to, uh, 'you know'?" and "Do you have protection?"—with a few Oh Yeahs and Oh Gods along the way. Brenda was pretty sure "Do you want to, 'you know'?" was nowhere near the level of detail Jeff had in mind.

Jeff wasn't the kind of guy who said, "Nice dress"; his compliments usually ran to whole sentences. O.k., he had said "Nice dress" once, but she had been in the shower at the time. That was another thing she liked. Jeff wasn't afraid to be silly.

Right now, he sat next to her looking serious. "Brenda? Thank you for letting me be your first."

"Um," she said. "You know . . . I thought I told . . ."

"Oh, I know you've had sex before. I meant letting me be your first to talk sex with. It's an honor." He gave her a flirtatious look. "Also seriously hot."

Seriously hot, Brenda thought, was the look he gave her. And his hands. His very skilled hands, and his even more skilled. . . . Well, he had lots of, um, skills. She snorted wryly.

"Funny?"

"Just laughing at myself. How can I talk about sex to you when I can't even talk about it in the privacy of my own head?" said Brenda.

"Ah," said Jeff, reaching for his backpack. "*Voici*! Resources. I

21

went online and found this." He handed her a sheaf of paper.

"'1001 Ways to Please Your Lover'?"

"You could read from it." He had that wicked expression again. "To build vocabulary."

She looked at the list, felt her cheeks warm. But she didn't want to stop. She made herself turn the page. "Read to you?"

"Read, talk, as long as it's out loud." He shifted his weight. She was intensely aware of his nearness, his heat. "Because you have such a sexy voice," he said.

"I'm going to blush if I read these."

"And such a sexy blush."

"Flattery!"

"Not flattery if it's true."

"You really want me to read this?"

"Maybe not all two dozen pages, but I'd like it very much if you'd read me some. But only if it feels o.k. to you to do it."

"I think . . . it's going to feel weird. But an o.k. kind of weird. And how will I know if I like it if I don't try?"

He said solemnly, "Exactly. You may discover that you are a virtuoso sex reader."

"Funny, that wasn't on any of those aptitude tests."

"Astronaut, cowgirl, and chocolate quality inspector weren't either. I'm not surprised they overlooked your incredibly sexy voice. Or your incredibly sexy. . . ." His gaze roamed down her body slowly. "Should I list from top to bottom, or alphabetically?"

"I should say reverse alphabetically, just to make you work hard!" she teased.

"You know I work hard," he said. "I work pretty well when I'm not hard, too." He swirled his tongue along his lips in a positively lewd motion.

"Yes," Brenda said demurely, "you do. You're very versatile."

"Damn right. Inspired, too. Don't forget inspired." He reached out, took her hand, and kissed her palm. "So. This list of possible sexual acts."

"A couple impossible ones, too. Guess I better pick wisely, huh? Be careful what I wish for?"

"Hey, this is just practicing saying stuff out loud. No obligation, no salesman will call. Whatever you read, I won't assume that's what you want to do, today or ever. Unless you tell me so. Explicitly," he said, looking at her that way again.

"Oh-ho, I begin to comprehend the outlines of your fiendish plan." She wasn't sure whether what she felt was nervous self-consciousness or pleasure. Or both, she thought suddenly; it could even be both. "Going to make me ask for what I want, eh?"

"What can I say?" he said. "I love the way you blush. Actually, I love the way you blush while continuing to do whatever you're blushing about."

"So I read until—what? You expire of frustration?"

"I prefer to call it 'erotic suspense'." He grinned. "Here's the game: You read something. I'll say, 'Captain, may I?' If you say, 'No, you may not,' I'll just lie here and savor your voice."

"Yeah, right," she said, amused. "You'll just lie there and look sexy at me until I jump on you to keep from going mad."

"Ooh," he said, appreciatively. "Good idea. Captain, may I?"

"No, you may not," she said, mock-sternly. "Well, not for at least fifteen minutes. I plan to make you suffer."

"Do your worst," he said, reclining, and stretching his arms over his head like a cat in sunshine.

O.k., she thought, if that's how we're playing. She looked for a big one; some people jump into the deep end of the pool if they're going in at all. "'Slide your tongue between the wet folds of her labia, savoring the taste of her excitement.'" Well, she wouldn't die of

23

blushing, even if she felt like a glowing coal.

"Whoa. You don't mess around." His voice was a purr. "Captain, may I?"

"No, you may not," she said, watching him.

He grinned. "Thank you, ma'am, may I please have another?"

She laughed, and chose at random. "'Trail kisses from the nape of her neck all the way to the base of her spine.'"

"Captain, may I?"

"No, you may not." It sounded nice. Maybe she should make a note for later.

"'Lie on your back, offering your erect cock to ride in whatever way pleases her.'" Hmm. Interesting idea. Two interesting ideas, actually. Possibly three. She was distracted from numbering possibilities by Jeff's face.

He bit his lip gently and looked at her through half-lidded eyes. "Captain, may I?"

"No, you may not." Inspired by his expression, she added, "Yet."

"Oh! Captain, you tease!"

"Erotic suspense, I think you said?"

"Captain, ma'am, you are an excellent tease," he said happily.

By the time she reached, "'Delicately bite her nipples—or let her bite yours,'" he was breathing hard. By "'Pretend you're in an X-rated pirate story; do some well-lubed plundering,'" they both were. At "'Touch your cock for her; make yourself come while she watches,'" he groaned aloud.

"'Reveal to her the word or words that turn you on the most,'" she said.

"Captain, may I?"

"I think you'd better."

"The sexiest word is 'yes'. Because it means you're doing what you're doing on purpose, with me, because you want to. Knowing

24

that," he said, "is the biggest turn-on. And I only know if you tell me."

She held his gaze. "Kiss me," she said.

"Captain, may I?"

She looked deep into his eyes, said, "Yes," and saw the pleasure rising through him. I am doing this on purpose, she thought, reaching for him, and the pleasure rose up in her own body with surprising strength. "Yes," she said again, coming down to cover his parted lips with her own. They kissed hungrily, saying "Yes," into each other's mouths. Her heart was beating so fast she thought they would both fall upward, into the sky.

They ran out of afternoon before they ran out of list.

"'Take off your clothes, slowly; let her watch you strip for her pleasure.'"

"Captain, may I?"

"That one definitely goes on the list."

"Mmm," he agreed, rubbing his cheek against her shoulder. "So, how do you like this talking about sex stuff?"

"I like. I definitely like. We should do this again."

"Anytime," he said.

"Maybe next time you should take a turn as Captain."

"Ooh," he said, looking at her speculatively. "Captain, may I?"

At the rumble of pleasure in his voice, Brenda felt a quiver deep inside. She considered the possibilities. Her lips curled into a long, lazy smile. "Yes, I think you may."

Power Game

By Marlo Gayle

Their asses were mine. They were broken, ready to submit. They couldn't hold my stare, my passion, my strength. They couldn't handle any more from me. I had them, and I could make them do what I wanted. My muscles flexed, twitched. Sweat drenched my t-shirt, the cool air causing my skin to tingle. I dug my cleats into the soft ground—I could almost feel the blades of grass on my soles.

"Hike!"

Sundeep took the ball from the center, his waist-length black hair done up in a top knot and covered as per Sikh custom. His long thin frame fluidly dancing a couple of Gene Kelly steps back. Two steps back . . . to me. I took the ball from his gracefully outstretched hand. I thought I heard several of my opponents moan as I cradled the ball and thrust myself into them. I felt their arms, their legs, their wills give from my contact, their bodies succumbing to mine. I could taste the mix of sweat and fear. They gave in to me and I took them . . .

"Damn, man, you were a beast out there," Sundeep said after the pickup game, as he traded the cloth covering his hair for a more formal turban.

"I just wanted it more," was my clichéd but honest response.

My passion, however, had a price. I knew I would be sore and stiff beyond movement. Dirt clung to my legs, sweat stung my eyes. I made my way back home. A hot shower would be a temporary delay to my upcoming muscular hangover. I had barely closed the door when I started peeling off my clothes. My t-shirt fell with a wet "clomp" to the floor. The skin around my chest and abs drank the air around their newly exposed flesh. My nipples got hard with the chill.

I slid off my cleats and my socks, my feet thankful for the release. My shorts and briefs were last to go, the cool air on my ass making my cock stir slightly. I reached the shower and turned on the faucet. Steam rose as needles of water shot from the shower head. The water caressed my body, warming my arms and legs, soothing my tired flesh. I lathered up my chest, my arms, the smooth skin on my freshly shaven head. I let the water rush over me, cleanse me. I soaped up my cock, my pubic hair foaming with lather. I ran the soap between my ass cheeks. A shudder ran through my body as my fingers ran past the small pucker within. I was getting lost in the pleasure of the moment when I heard a sigh.

"Oh, hi, Joani," I said, startled. "Uh, how long have you been standing there?"

"Long enough," she answered with a tease in her voice. "I, uh, followed your scent after I came in."

"Gosh, why did I ever give you the keys to my place?" I smart-assed.

"I'm a good lay," she smart-assed back. Her quick wit was one of the things I loved about her. "Another tackle football game with the boys?"

"Yup, they needed a little pain. I'm more than happy to give it to them."

"You and your full contact," she said in mock disgust. "You're going to end up arthritic and crippled."

"You'd better enjoy me until then," I countered.

"I plan to. Meet me in the bedroom, and I'll see what I can do for your muscles."

I couldn't get out of the tub fast enough. I made a half effort toweling off. My feet left wet prints all the way into the bedroom. Joani squatted upon the bed. She had mischief on her mind.

"Come here, lay down, and I'll rub you down." No arm-twisting was needed. I immediately flopped, naked, face down on the bed.

"Flip over!" she commanded. "I want to do your front first."

I rolled over and looked deeply into her eyes. I began to lose myself inside them.

"Put your arms above your head." I obliged. She climbed on top of me and straddled my chest. I quickly realized she had no panties on under the skirt she wore. Her pussy was warm and wet against my chest. I reached up to caress her legs.

"Now behave and keep your arms up!" I put my arms back where they were. She slid further up my chest and leaned forward. Her breasts smothering me through her blouse. I felt her tie something silky around my wrists.

"What are you doing?" I knew what she was doing and her smile for an answer told me she knew I knew. She fastened both wrists to the bed frame and, still straddling me, slid back down towards my waist. My cock was hard as the tensed muscles in my arms.

"Now comes the fun part," she teased.

Button by button she slowly took off her blouse. I didn't blink, my eyes fixated on the delicate dance of fingers on fabric, exposing her wonderful flesh. Her beautiful bra, black, almost menacing, the only barrier between her nipples and my steady gaze. She tore down that wall quickly, deftly removing her support with a flick of her fingers. Her skirt, the only fabric left on her magnificent body, stretched across me, spread between her strong legs. It served as another bond, using her weight to force me into the bed. I became even harder; my cock wanted what was under that skirt.

Joani reached over to the table by the bed and grabbed the massage oil. She took a palmful and warmed it by rubbing her hands together, releasing the spicy aroma. She placed her warm slick fingers onto my chest and firmly began to rub. The reality of the game had begun to show itself in my muscles, and Joani's skilled fingers teased this soreness to her delight—and mine. It was just enough pain to endure. Enough to know I was being touched, worked on by someone who knew what she was doing. She was in control and I relaxed into it, her fingers firmly blazing trails through my aching flesh. I moaned with pleasure and pain. Joani beamed in achievement as she milked each cry, the conductor bringing music out of her instrument. I sank, I let her play me.

She slowly, achingly returned to my chest, where she paid particular attention to my rather hard nipples. She gleefully pinched them, eliciting a yelp from me in response. She moved down to my abs, where she carefully drew borders around each muscle with her fingers. She moved to my inner thighs where she enjoyed touching me softly, making my dick even harder.

"Please," I begged. The torture of touch had brought me to my boiling point as my arms strained against their silken bondage. She smiled in response, her fingers slowly making their way up my groin. When she delicately took the head of my penis between her thumb and index finger and pinched, I knew . . .

I was hers.

Sex Club Hopping in Paris

By Lisa Archer

The man peered at me through a crack in the door. "Do you know what kind of club this is?"

"Yes." I had found it searching Google for clubs *échangistes*. These "swingers' clubs" were also known as *clubs libertines*, which sounded like an invention of the Marquis de Sade: a club for committing acts of unbridled lust and defiling innocent youths.

Smiling a mouthful of stained teeth, the man opened the door. Several men at a dimly lit bar grinned at me, leaning over each other to get a better view. The sign above the door read: 50 Euro per couple, 80 Euro per single man. It didn't mention women.

"How much is the cover?"

The man with stained teeth smiled. "For you, it is free."

A disco ball threw circles of colored light up the spiral staircase. The dance floor was empty. Men lolled around in oxford shirts and khakis. They circled me, exchanging wary glances. One of them—shirtless, with wiry muscles—blew me a wet kiss and ran his forefinger under my chin. Another danced almost on top of me, like a dog jerking himself off on my leg. I recoiled, accustomed to San Francisco's private sex parties, where "Ask before you touch" was the rule. These parties forbade street clothes and required nudity, fetish wear, or lingerie. Finally I saw a woman in the middle of a throng of men. A man in an oxford shirt and navy blue socks knelt between her thighs, fucking her, his white briefs around his ankles. What was it with the oxford shirts and khakis? I couldn't imagine anything less sexy. There were no other women in sight.

Perhaps women came here for gangbangs. I was not into gangbangs in foreign "libertine clubs," where people might have a much different idea of what a consensual gangbang meant. I was ready to leave.

"Do you feel comfortable here?" asked young man in a bright blue button-down shirt. He was handsome in a pale way, with aquiline nose and brown hair, parted on the side. I sat down next to him, thankful for someone to talk to.

"I wish there were more women."

He nodded. "This is a special club. They allow single people. Most clubs are for couples. It's unusual to see a single woman here."

I shrugged. "I would rather have gone to go to a club for couples, but I leave Paris tomorrow. I didn't know any men I could take with me."

"If you want, we could leave here and go to a club for couples. I am called Etienne."

I looked at him. I prefer more bohemian men, and it isn't every day I climb into strangers' cars to go to "libertine clubs." I wasn't sure I could distinguish between sexy and crazy in a foreign culture. But, sex-starved, I decided to go for it.

We walked to his car in the crisp night air.

"I just broke up with my girlfriend," he said, unlocking the door of a blue Peugeot with a baby seat in the back. The baby seat made me feel more comfortable. It suggested he had something to lose.

"Did you used to go to clubs for couples with your girlfriend?"

"No. She didn't know about them."

I was surprised: I knew lots of couples in S.F. who went to sex parties together. "Then who did you go to clubs for couples with?"

"Women I met at clubs—like you."

"Did you ever think of telling her about the clubs?"

"No. I made that mistake once with a girl I was dating. She said she never wanted to see me again. Then she told all my friends, 'He goes to those kinds of clubs.' I told them, 'She's lying.' That was that. I never saw her again. I like the anonymity. I think that's what I like about the clubs."

I listened, fascinated by his double life. He was one of those people who share their darkest secrets with a stranger on a train they'll never see again.

We pulled up alongside a restaurant with a red carpet leading to the entrance. A valet opened the car door for me.

"This is it?" I asked, having never seen a sex club with a red carpet and a valet. The doorman beckoned us into a dining hall with black walls, high ceilings, and hundreds of red leather chairs. The tables were empty, except for a party of three elderly women eating dessert with their lap dogs. The French bring their dogs to restaurants— apparently to sex clubs too.

On a sofa by the bar, we kissed for the first time. Etienne was a good kisser, but something cold and wet was probing my thigh. I glanced down. A well-groomed Shih Tzu regarded us with interest, wagging his tail.

Etienne pulled back, quickly buttoning his shirt. "They don't like us to do this in the restaurant. Let's go upstairs. That's where the club is."

Upstairs a dozen couples mingled in the dimly lit play space. The women dressed in slinky black lingerie, while the men wore requisite oxford shirts and khakis. The place seemed clean, but had a distinct lack of condoms, lube, gloves and other safer sex supplies.

We kissed on a black vinyl-covered bed. Suddenly a hand crept up my thigh. A large man, wearing only a v-neck sweater, was prodding my pussy with his bare hands—which had probably fingered every woman in the room. I grabbed his wrist and pushed him away, swearing to get a full STD check as soon as I got home. He generously offered to fuck me without a condom. I was graciously declining, when a woman with spiky two-tone hair crept up on my pussy—

cooing at it, as if it were a small pet—and eyed me as if to ask, "Does it bite?"

"She wants to eat you," said Etienne. I nodded, confused by foreign sounds and gestures.

The woman marveled at my cunt as if it were a saintly relic, too fragile and holy to touch. Finally she lowered her head, slurping enthusiastically. Etienne kissed me. A black woman lay down beside us. A black man, naked and uncut, slid his cock into her and ran his hands over Etienne's ass. The woman with spiky hair whispered sweet nothings to my pussy in French. I couldn't understand her, since her mouth was full. But soon I was coming in waves. The woman glanced up at me with a worshipful expression and batted away the man in the v-neck as he tried to fuck her doggy style.

When I finished coming, I glanced around for the woman. She was already busy fucking Etienne. I raced off to the shower.

When I came back, Etienne pulled me down next to him and kissed my feet, working his way up my legs. The black couple lay down next to us again and stroked us as they made love. Etienne put on a condom and slid into me with long, slow thrusts. I came again. Then Etienne came, his back breaking out in a sheen of sweat. I kissed him, licking the sweat off his neck.

We slipped away to the locker room, showered, dressed, and went downstairs.

Etienne paid the bill, flirting with the pretty coat check girl. I wondered if she'd be the next woman he'd take to a club for couples. For all I knew, he was asking her right then.

The next morning, as I lugged my suitcase out of the hotel, I saw Etienne reading a newspaper in the window of a café. The woman across from him held a baby in her arms. He looked up and pretended not to notice me.

After all, he led a double life.

Speaking in Tongues

By Edward Beggs

*D*riving through this forest country of scented Douglas firs reminds me of Norma, a woman I knew years ago. Norma was not strikingly beautiful but she was sexually audacious. Like her mother, she was a large woman, not fat, but tall and ample bodied. She had fair skin, honey-blond hair, blue eyes, and full, sensuous lips. Her blushing smile was disarming and her seductive come-ons seemed as dangerous as live cobras. As her pastor in those days, I was impressed with her quick mind but was guarded against her flirtatious overtures.

Before leaving that community Norma invited me to go horseback riding. As Norma saddled the horses I was wondering if she had any plans to fulfill her sexual ambitions with me. As we began the ride, Norma's horse made menacing moves toward mine. The striking hoof missed the shoulder of my horse but nicked my left ankle. My ankle was seriously hurt. The ride in the isolated woods would have to remain a titillating fantasy.

Traveling in this mountain forest years later stirs up old memories of Norma. I wonder how her face and body have changed. I had obtained her phone number from her mother and I decided to act on this stimulating impulse.

Norma had in previous years married a preacher who ranted against a special taboo. Like many church denominations, this man defined himself by what he tried to forbid. As the Mormons prohibited Cokes and coffee, the Methodists fine wines and beer, the Southern Baptists dancing and rock and roll, the Catholics self-pleasuring and premarital sex, and the extinct Shakers sex, even in

marriage, so Norma's preacher man and his Covenant
of the Strict Path defined his denominational brand, like the
rest of them, by forbidding an obvious pleasure. To insure product
differentiation, however, he would specialize. He would be against
oral sex!

Rubbing up nightly against these preacherly prohibitions
Norma's curiosity about oral pleasures grew intense. The Reverend
became increasingly uncomfortable as the more he admonished the
congregation to avoid the vile and filthy practice he could only indirectly discuss from the pulpit, Norma was
nibbling closer in her adventurous quest for variation in the holy bed
of matrimony. He banished her from his bed, expelled her from the
Strict Path and had the marriage annulled.

When I finally reconnect with Norma she is living by herself in a
trailer on a horse ranch near the highway I'm traveling. I left my pas-
toral persona in the dust years ago and am thrilled at the prospect of
seeing Norma face to face. Hearing my maroon van driving up on
the gravel she steps out of her door, looks directly at me, smiles and
says, without blushing, "I'm so happy to see you again!"

She wears faded jeans and a long-sleeved blue flannel shirt. She
likes the beard I've grown since I knew her. We greet each other
with a tentative hug, our first. There is no one looking over our
shoulders and no professional roles to uphold. We are both free
agents.

We're also cold!

Norma breaks free, takes my hand and leads me into the trailer
where a wood stove throws out enough heat to convert a freedom-
loving winter hobo to the joys of domestic servitude. We talk and
laugh about her former attempts to seduce me and her equally frus-
trating times in the Strict Path. We are shy and nervous about what is
about to happen. I shiver now, not from the outside cold, but from

35

sheer nerve-wracking sexual excitement.

Demonstrating amazing restraint, she suggests we take a horse-back ride to see Calamity Point. Norma saddles the horses, and with nary a kick to anyone's ankle we ride off. We wade the horses through Rush Creek and pink-tinged heather. We climb to an overview of a wide valley of sage and blackened rock surrounded by snow-topped mountains—Calamity Point, a vista view of ancient volcanic eruptions. Eventually we turn the horses homeward and they take us swiftly back to the cozy warmth of the wood stove.

I kick off my shoes and pull off her scuffed brown boots. She lies back on the front room couch and her blond hair splays across the pillow. I snuggle next to her body and enjoy her scent. Like a pony's velvet lips nibbling clover blossoms, I touch my lips to hers. After massaging her neck and shoulders I rest my palm on the soft mound of her shirt-covered breast.

She whispers: "Oh, God!"

I unzip her jeans and move down to her feet to grab her cuffs and pull them off with gentle tugs. Moving my fingers under the elastic, I slip off her white cotton panties. I inhale the awesome scent from her cunt. With hands on her knees I spread her warm thighs and move between them. Parting her labia with a moist tongue I introduce her to the liberating joys of the oral tradition. Her whispers to God have now become loud pleas of "Oh, Jesus!"

Burying my face in this primal place makes the tick-tock mark-ing of time irrelevant. I alternate between slow tongue strokes up and down her entire labia to rapid flicking of her clitoris. This goes on and on until her breathing becomes quicker and deeper. As she begins to thrash around and arch her back I hold her thighs tight to maintain contact with my tongue.

Her moans deepen and seem to come from such a primitive place they scare me. I feel her shudder, hear her scream, and as her taut body collapses onto the bed, I lift my head from her vulva. I feel a different kind of pleasure in seeing her satisfaction. Eyes closed, she rests quietly.

Now her eyelids lift and rising on one elbow she smiles broadly and exclaims: "Wow! No wonder the church didn't want us to do that."

Birthday Rap

By Kecia

On my birthday morning I was awakened by the burning desire to make love. My partner had his children visiting and so we didn't sleep together the evening before. As I lay there, the fire in my loins throbbed and grew with each moment. I decided to go to the room where he was sleeping to see if I could get some goodies before the girls woke up. I quietly crept in and began nuzzling his ear and neck. I whispered in his ear, "Can you come and play this morning before I leave?" He smiled and said yes.

Even though we have made love while the children were sleeping before, he was not on the same page and could not get his mind or his member to task. Now I do know that he loves sex with me and I crave him all the time, but sometimes he can be in his head and cannot get out enough to perform, if you know what I mean. Because of time and a pending appointment I was forced to abandon my efforts to help him cum around.

It was a beautiful summer day. Children were playing; men greeted me with approval as I approached the bus stop. I thought about how badly I wanted to fuck.

While I was standing there I noticed a car that came around with a gentleman who looked at me as if he knew me. He said hello and asked if I would come to the car and talk to him. I said no, he would have to get out of the car and come talk to me where I stood. He pulled over, got out of his car, and approached me. He was a handsome younger man, neatly dressed in a sweat suit that showed his well-built frame. He asked if he could give me a ride somewhere. I told him I was running late and would appreciate the lift. I got in the car, and we started talking. He told me he had seen me as he passed and had doubled back to see who I was. He said he was attracted to my sumptuous behind, which he noticed as I was standing there.

As we drove he put his hand on my thigh and raised my dress to reveal my thighs. He caressed my leg and then I noticed his hard-on. It was quite large, and I could feel the moisture growing between my legs as he stroked me. I'm a sucker for a big dick so I pulled it out of his pants and started touching it as he drove. When we stopped at a light I swear I thought the woman at the bus stop could see me stroking his huge beautiful cock. By now my mouth was watering. I wanted to suck his dick right then and there, with the woman looking at me. (I'm an exhibitionist sometimes too!)

We were just a few blocks from my destination and I had to compose myself quickly. When we got there he said he would wait for me. As I got out of the car he grabbed me and planted a big kiss on my lips and pressed his hard dick against me. He said he would sit there and smoke a blunt while he waited.

When I came back, he said he had to make a stop and asked if I had time to go with him. I said sure and off we went. We caressed each other till I thought I was going to explode. He finished his errands and said let's go for a ride, I want to fuck you so bad I can't wait. We stopped to pick up some condoms and something to quench our thirst. We stopped at a park up in the hills, a rugged place with no people around that we could see, so we got out of the car and proceeded to look for someplace in the brush where we could satisfy our lust. We looked around and didn't see anyplace that was easily accessible, so we went back to his car. As he opened the door for me and I sat down I could not help but grab his hard cock. I pulled it out and began sucking wildly on it. The huge head on his cock felt good to my tongue and I couldn't stop sucking even with a car approaching.

By now I'm on fire. I told him there was a picnic table just down the road from where we were. Let's go there, I said, and he obliged. When we got to the spot he placed a towel from the trunk of his car on the table. He pulled up my dress and began squeezing and caressing my ass. He licked it and kissed it then turned me around. He said if he hit it from the back he knew he would not be able to hold on. He lifted me onto the table, pulled his sweat pants down and put a condom on that beautiful huge cock. He pressed the head of his dick against my lips and rubbed it against them until they parted to allow his entry, then thrust his cock deep into my pussy. I gasped as he entered me. I thought I was going to lose my mind as he stroked my pussy with his large, long, firm dick. I was so wet; as he slammed his big cock in and out of my juicy pussy I could see his groin becoming more and more moist.

We hadn't noticed the truck coming up as we were consumed with the pleasure we were producing. When we did it was right there upon us—all we could do was stop and hold each other, with me writhing and squirming on his dick and his firm round ass exposed for all to see. After the truck went by we were at it again, thrusting and squirming all over each other until I screamed with ecstasy. I came in big sporadic waves of pleasure, nearly collapsing from the intensity. He never missed a stroke and held my ass as he continued to push his pulsing manness deeper and deeper. Then with a huge scream of his own he exploded, his cock pulsing and throbbing as he lay limp against me. We lay there against each other for a while until we got our composure.

He had told me earlier that he was a rapper and was producing a video for his latest project. I had not paid him any attention when he told me this; I had his dick in my hand and sucking it on my mind. I had no idea until he broke out rapping this cool piece. I mean he was totally inspired and performed it as if he were on stage. Then he showed me his CD and played the joint he had just performed.

After this I can only imagine what his next CD will be like.

Leave a Message

BY SAGE VIVANT

Springtime makes me restless. I adore and despise it for this reason. As I lay in bed that morning, running my hand along the
sheet where John's body had warmed it, I squirmed with sensory
echoes of the taut muscles in his chest and the firm fullness of his
backside.

Ignoring my conscience, I reached across the mattress toward the
phone on the nightstand. As I dialed, a subtle breeze suggested previously unthinkable scenarios as it danced along my long, exposed legs.
I heard the phone on the other end ring once, twice, three times
before it clicked over to voice mail. The sound of his voice brought
mischief to mind and at the sound of the beep, I lay back on the bed
and spoke.

"Hi, baby. It's Becky. I'm just lying here, wondering how I'm
going to get through the day without the feel of your skin against
mine. I'm not even out of bed yet and I'm already wet."
I giggled, suddenly nervous. I'd never left a message like this for John
before—it was his personal voice mail yet I knew that he often
picked up his messages when he was with clients or out in public, so
I didn't want to make him uncomfortable. But now I could only
think about all manner of phallic pleasures.

I hung up because I was uncertain about what else to say and I
wasn't sure I should go into any more detail. He'd get a kick out of
the message, I thought to myself as I headed for the shower.

The thought of John's round butt cheeks in my hands and his
beautiful manhood in my mouth or between my legs made shower-
ing a fairly futile experience. But I didn't want to come in the

shower. If I couldn't have John in person, I'd at least share with him by phone what he was missing. When I emerged from the steamy bathroom, still damp and aroused beyond reason, I curled up on my unmade bed and picked up the phone again.

"Hi, John. It's me again. I just got out of the shower and I'm afraid I'm not at all clean. My pussy just keeps dripping for you. I don't even know if I can get dressed. I mean, what could I put on that will help?" I walked over to my closet, the section where I kept my best lingerie. "Let's see. . . . There's this beautiful copper teddy. You remember it, don't you? It's the one with the cutouts at the cups. Do you remember when you sucked my nipples when I wore it? You said you liked it because it made my hair look richer. Auburn, I think you said. Anyway, it keeps my breasts free so if I wear that under clothing, I think the fabric will just rub against them and I'll be more turned on than ever.

"There's always the merry widow with the thong. I think you like that one, too. It pushes my breasts up high, like I'm a bawdy maid from the Renaissance! The thong strokes me when I walk, especially if I'm already wet. No, that won't do.

"I don't think I have anything that's going to help, John. I wish I could design something," I said, walking back to the bed and settling in at the head of it. "If I could design something to wear today, I'd make something with cups the size and shape of your hands. The panty would be silky but it would be lined with little miniatures of your tongue so that you could lap away at me all day. Mmmm, that would be lovely."

My hand was between my legs now and my fingers moved along my moist folds like I imagined his would if he were with me. "John, I'm playing with myself now. I'm sorry to leave you this message, but I'm so aroused, I don't know what else to do. I'm terribly wet right now. Listen." I put the phone to my pussy and let him listen to the squishing sounds I created with a few carefully placed movements of my fingers. Once I knew my orgasm was close, I moved the phone back to my mouth.

"Oh, John. It's your mouth pleasuring me. Oh! Yeeesssss!"

I really did imagine his handsome face between my grateful legs. When my vaginal walls quivered with the after-effects of my lusty exploration, I remembered that I was leaving a message and should probably sign off soon. "I'm going to hang up now, sweetie, but that doesn't mean I've stopped thinking about you."

The restful glow of my orgasm was only the beginning of my hunger that day. I indulged myself, though, stretching cat-like as my body recovered from its little death. My imagination would not be ignored, however, and it raced with ideas for the evening. I gave each idea considerable thought as I lay there, naked, fondling my breasts and even occasionally sucking one to stave off the wild, incessant horniness that consumed me. I waited an hour or so before I phoned again.

"John, it's Becky again. As the day progresses, I'm afraid I'm still not able to do anything other than think about you and those luscious buttcheeks of yours. I'm thinking I'll go over to that seedy little sex shop on Melford Road, you know the one with the leather in the window? I wouldn't buy anything too serious, you understand, but the idea of some tight black leather stretched across my breasts really gets me hot.

"You should have called me today. You should have whispered sweet nothings to me and made me come on the phone. You should have promised me that you would cover me with kisses. But you didn't do any of that, so now I get to have my way with you.

"I'm going to bend you over and make you wait to discover what I'll do next. Will I slap you with my bare hands? Will I use the whip? Or maybe I'll just grab a wooden spoon and leave red outlines of its shape on your gorgeous rear end.

"There's only one way for you to know what I'm going to do, John. Come home early and find out."

I hung up and got dressed right away. I had to get to Melford Road before that store closed.

His Hands

By Greta Christina

This is what she thinks about, when she thinks about him. She doesn't think about his eyes, like she likes to tell herself; or about his lips, like she'd tell her friends if they knew about him; or about his cock, like she tells him when she's in a good mood. She thinks about his hands.

When he wants her, it's always his hands that go first. Brushing lightly against her face. Sneaking up on her thigh. Massaging the back of her neck, and then inching down over her collarbones to entice her breasts. His hands are smart—smarter than he is, probably—and his hands are sweet when they want to be, and they can make her feel calm and drifty, safe and befriended.

But it isn't these nice sweet things she thinks about. His hands also do things that make her blush when she remembers, things that make her flinch and quickly look for something to stare at on the floor, convinced that anyone who sees her can read her mind. When she thinks about his hands, these are the things she thinks about.

She thinks about his hands pressing her against the wall, one hand pinning her shoulders, the other sliding up her skirt, pushing between her legs, reaching for her clit like it belongs to him. No, not like it belongs to him. Like a thief. Like he knows it doesn't belong to him and is taking it anyway.

She thinks about his hands pressing her thighs apart, again like a thief, like a cat burglar opening a window and climbing inside. She thinks about his hand on the back of her neck, his fingers coiling in her hair and tightening; she thinks about his other hand gripping her by the wrist, guiding her own hand between his legs, making her feel his swelling crotch. She thinks about his hands on her arms, shaking, impatient, maneuvering her body into place.

She thinks about his fingers spreading her lips open down there, prying her apart, exposing her clit and studying it fervently as if he's reading her soul. When he opens her up like that, she feels like he is revealing her soul, like her soul has been hiding in her clit and he's discovered it at last: her true soul, the selfish one, the dirty one, the one that wants to quit her job and abandon her friends and family and spend the rest of her life on her back, on her hands and knees, pressed against the wall, with his hand between her legs.

She thinks he's a bad idea. She thinks she doesn't love him. She thinks that if she loved him, she wouldn't feel so dirty all the time. She thinks that if she loved him, she'd think about his eyes, his lips, even his cock, at least sometimes. She thinks that if she loved him, she wouldn't be spending every spare moment thinking about his hands.

She thinks about his hands. And finds her own hand knocking at his door.

Restaurant Opening

By Melanie Votaw

He failed to notice how sexy she looked in her little black dress, as always. She had given up long ago trying to elicit attention from her husband. His only interest seemed to be his work, and it did not seem to bother him at all that they were essentially living a celibate life. Even though a private investigator had failed to find any evidence of an affair, she could never get a straight answer from him as to why he had lost his appetite for sex.

She continued to keep in shape and dress sexy anyway. It made her feel good, and she enjoyed the attention she received from the men she passed by on the street or met at the office. Although she had never cheated on her husband, she was seriously considering it. How long could any woman live like this? She knew she would have to make some decision soon, or her passion would simply die.

Once a week they went out to dinner, and he chattered away as if there was nothing amiss in their relationship. This particular evening, he sat next to her at the small square table. After dessert, her husband was saying something about the beautiful mosaic tabletop when she noticed the handsome young man sitting at the table directly across from them. He was with a lovely young woman but seemed to have no more interest in his dinner companion than she had in hers. He looked up and caught her staring. When he smiled, she quickly looked away.

Terribly bored and in need of adventure, she suddenly got a brainstorm. The man was sitting in just the right place to see her legs under the table. And unless she turned her head, the woman with him would not be able to see.

She excused herself to the ladies' room, where she tucked her panties into her bag. When she sat back down, she feigned a renewed interest in her husband's topics of conversation, while keeping her peripheral vision locked on the young man. Whenever the waiters left the area, she moved her legs back and forth, opening and closing, opening and closing. Just when she thought he would never look, and just when she had almost talked herself out of this madness, he saw! His eyes widened, his breath obviously quickened, and he abruptly looked guiltily back at his companion.

Continuing to say "um hmm" to her husband at appropriate moments, she kept an eye out for the moment when the man could find a chance to look back at her. When the young woman excused herself to the ladies' room, the man turned in his chair nonchalantly to look straight under their table. She spread her legs wider and held them open. Then, she brought her hand down to her lap and ran her finger up and down her labia. When she inserted her finger into her vagina, his mouth opened in response, and he squirmed in his seat.

Her husband continued his conversation mostly with himself, oblivious to what was happening under the table. She kept looking back in the direction of the ladies' room, ready to stop as soon as the young woman was on her way back.

When she pulled her finger out, it was covered in white cream. This experience was making her wetter than she had been in a long time! She lifted her finger and quickly put it in her mouth, licking it clean. The young man's eyes stayed fixed on her.

A waiter started their way with the check, and she reluctantly closed her legs. When the waiter was gone, the man looked at her longingly, his eyes begging her to continue. She opened her legs again and returned her finger to her lap, spreading her juices all over her clitoris and labia. Her passion was building, and she longed to bring herself to orgasm. But, her husband placed the cash in the check folder, and she knew it was almost time to leave. She let the man watch her clean her juicy finger with the cloth napkin on her table, after which she brought the napkin to her lap, running it along her pussy from bottom to top.

Squeezing the napkin in her right hand as her husband headed toward the door, she stopped briefly by the young man, dropping the napkin on his table without looking at him.

She turned the corner, passing the young man's companion on the way back to his table, as she and her husband stepped out of the restaurant.

Gold

By Kelly DaCrioch

*T*here are times when your feet are set upon a shining path. When the stars float around your head and everything you touch turns to gold. Warm, malleable, sweet.

The night of Laura's birthday party was one of those times. It was late September, so different from the dark dreariness of a San Francisco August, and the wind off the bay chilled my skin. I was polarized, magnetized, following the pull of pure luck. In a way, it was too bad. Too much of a good thing all at once. Impossible to follow up on. The next time I saw Debra I was tired, actually had a terrible cold, but I kept our date anyway. After our first night—this night—I thought I could do no wrong.

I was wrong. Really wrong. Our first actual date was also our last.

But that night, Laura's birthday party—oh, my.

It was crowded, as all Laura's parties were, sixty people or more crushed into her Webster Street flat: expatriate East Coaster friends, the Marin Goth crowd, the science fiction bookstore crowd, the Upper and Lower Haight Street contingents, and Laura's lovers past, present, and future. I would be in the "past" category, which seemed to include about half the party.

I was answering an unanswerable riddle when I saw Debra come in the front door. Debra is tall and needs no ornament. In her gray down jacket and nondescript blue jeans, she towered above the press of dyed-black pineapple heads and bleached do's around her.

"What's the difference between an orange?" my friend Chris had asked me. A question to befuddle drunks, to elicit sputters and confused Ah, fuck yous. I looked across the room at Debra's reddish brown hair, curly and cut close, and the answer rose unbidden.

"One is red," I said slowly, "and the other is yellow. Excuse me."

I made my way through the crowded living room. Debra made her way towards me. We said hello, we chatted as the milling of the crowd jostled us together until the space between us was so small, if I had leaned forwards, I could have licked her slightly pointed, slightly upturned nose. She was precise, direct, interesting and charismatic. I was witty, charming, and sincere. I wish I could remember what the hell we said to each other.

We wandered through the party together. To the fridge for bottles of beer, leaning against the wall in the long Victorian hall that split the flat, crammed together on the couch with four drunk punks who eventually formed a successful swing band, then back through the kitchen, past the fridge and past Laura who leaned against the sink and said "Hey, sugar," with a knowing smile. We went out the back door and on to the stairwell, in the airshaft between Laura's building and the next.

We leaned against the railing, which overlooked the trash cans and the side door to the garage. Above us in a rectangle cutout of sky, a few of the brightest stars showed through the glowing San Francisco mist.

My arm was around her waist. I felt her weight shift, her shoulder pressed under mine, and I kissed her broad, soft cheek. She turned her face towards me, her brows arched, and I kissed the space between them. Then a little lower, the bridge of her nose, then the tip. She tilted her face away from mine.

"How do I know it's not just the alcohol in you?"

"Because I've been attracted to you from the moment I first saw you last spring."

"When we all watched the Alice in Wonderland video?"

"When you first came in the door, and Laura introduced us, yes."

"You were going out with Laura then, right?"

"We broke up about a month later. But I hardly ever saw you around."

"Too bad." She tilted her head forward and I kissed her mouth. She kissed back. We stayed that way for a long time. My arms slid inside her jacket, warm around her back as the night air frosted the nape of my neck. I felt her breasts push against my chest, her left arm around my shoulders, her right hand reaching into my back pocket.

I glanced back toward the kitchen. Through the window above the sink I could see Laura, Chris, and other partygoers. One gestured toward the window and they all laughed. I unwrapped myself from Debra and pulled her with me into deeper shadow, against the wall. My back pressed against the old, damp planking and she spun so her back pressed into me. I caught her in my arms and she collapsed just the tiniest bit, letting me hold her up.

I arched forward and kissed her neck, chewed a while on her right ear. She let herself moan a little, rocked her body against mine, ground her ass into my crotch. My hands cupped her breasts as I continued to chew her neck, first through her sweatshirt, then through her blouse, then under her blouse as I pinched and kneaded her nipples through her bra. She made a gasping sound and pushed back harder against me. I gripped her tighter in turn.

"I want to," she breathed, "but . . . "

I released her neck. "I know."

"It's just that . . . "

"I know," I said again, gently. "It's not the right time for that, or the right place." I looked back at the kitchen window, saw the heads bobbing and weaving. "But still . . . "

My right hand slid inside her belt, down past the elastic of her underwear, and I felt how wet she was. Her knees buckled and I caught her, my left arm around her ribs as my right hand slid up and down, as much as the tightness of her jeans allowed. I rested my chin on her shoulder, and kissed her cheek again.

"I can at least give you this," I whispered.

She didn't answer, but reached down and released the clasp on her belt, unfastened the top button of her jeans. My fingers reached deeper, past the lips of her cunt to where she was slippery and warm, and used the slickness to massage her clitoris. She began to move, just a little, up and down, matching the rhythm of my fingers. My left arm squeezed her body closer and closer against me, my hand rubbed hard, and Debra began to chant "yes yes yes there, yes, there . . ." until she moaned "ohmygod" and fell back into me completely.

A little bit shyly, I took my right hand away, not sure of what to do with it. Debra refastened her jeans and belt, then leaned forward and kissed my lips again. Then she took my right hand in hers, still wet, and kissed that.

"Thank you," she said.

"It was truly my pleasure," I said.

"We'll have to do that again."

"I hope so. Soon."

But it was not to be. Maybe if I'd seen her the next day, or not seen her again for a month, but the timing was all wrong. Some days you are on the shining path and the gold is soft and warm in your hands, and all you can do is make the most of it while it lasts.

Chemistry

By Marcy Sheiner

I want to rub my body all over his, I thought, the minute I saw him standing in the entrance to the café. He was a huge man, about six foot three, maybe 230 pounds, with a deep golden tan and an unruly sun-bleached beard.

Startled and flushed, I buried my head behind a newspaper, dismayed that at the age of forty-four I could still cream in my panties at the mere sight of a total stranger. Besides, I'd spent four hours fucking the previous night—wasn't it enough? Then again, in all those hours I had failed to have an orgasm.

Brian and I had been seeing each other for several months. He was ten years younger than me and a good deal smaller in every way but one: he had a nine-inch cock. I liked his athleticism and staying power—he always fucked me long and hard—but I had never yet been able to come with him. I was starting to think that his physique had something to do with it: I like to be able to crawl all over a man without feeling like I'm crushing him. I'm no Barbie doll. I'm a fleshy, lusty lady who likes to take what she wants when she wants it, and I need a man who's solid enough to handle me. The stranger definitely looked like he could. Slowly I lowered my paper, and was surprised to find him staring at me.

I blushed and lowered my eyes. Now, how had he managed to zero in on me? I'd done nothing overt—yet an invisible thread of electricity crackled and joined us through a roomful of people. Some kind of indefinable chemistry was at work, the mysterious doings of a mysterious universe.

I turned to the astrology page and read my horoscope. "A new relationship will prove to be a challenge in your already complex life."

Beads of perspiration broke out on my forehead. I heard the scrape of a chair, and felt the stranger's powerful presence beside me before I even looked up to see his oceanic blue eyes boring into me.

"My name's Jake," he said, as if it were the most natural thing in the world. "Do you live around here?"

"Not too far," I said, finally meeting his gaze. Looking into those eyes, I became awash in a sea of desire. Pheromones fairly poured off Jake's body, making my nerve endings tingle and my fingertips ache with the need to touch him.

Jake ordered a slice of cake, which he pretty much inhaled in one fell swoop. He made small talk, the substance of which evaded me as I studied his hands, imagining them on my breasts. I wished I were the piece of cake in his hungry mouth.

"So," he said quite suddenly, "What do you want to do with me?"

A fiery blush spread up my neck and face. "You know what I want to do with you," I whispered.

"It's okay," Jake said. "Come on, let's get out of here."

He took my hand. Sheets of electricity ran from my fingertips up my arm, over my neck, down to my hot wet center. I struggled to maintain dignity, but I knew it was a losing battle.

I'd had dozens of lovers, some wonderful, some not, but if there was one thing they all had in common it was a basic gentleness. It suddenly occurred to me that I yearned to lose myself in a powerfully masculine man, but I'd been afraid to give in to this desire.

In my apartment, Jake's big hands roamed over my arms and breasts and hips with slow deliberation, as if taking possession. I dissolved into soft, yielding flesh. He kissed me, his mouth slightly open, his tongue elusive. We moved to the sofa and Jake continued kissing me, not letting his tongue enter my mouth. Then his hand crept under the elastic of my panties and his fingers toyed with my vaginal lips, parting them, pressing, teasing. Suddenly he plunged his fingers into my cunt and his tongue into my mouth both at the same moment. The incomparable shock of penetration was thrilling, and I allowed myself to melt down to the place I wanted to be, spreading my legs, kissing passionately. After a few minutes Jake pulled me on top of him. My cunt pressed against the bulge in his pants and I began to grind against it. Deftly he lifted my blouse, unhooked my bra and took my big tits into his mouth. I wept soundlessly, my pelvis on automatic, grinding a hot sexy dance.

Jake moved his mouth to my ear. "That's right, honey, grind it," he whispered encouragingly. In a moment I began to come—after knowing this man half an hour, I was totally uninhibited, writhing on top of his generous body.

After my orgasm subsided I sat up on him, opened his fly and pulled out his gorgeous prick. Jake put his fingers, musky with my juices, into my mouth and thrust them down my throat. I sank down to his cock, opened my mouth and took it in. "Suck it," he ordered. "Think about it touching your pussy. Think about the head teasing your cunt." He continued talking a literal blue streak, something that drives me crazy. His words spurred me on to more avid sucking.

He reached down with his hand and pulled his cock out of my mouth, rubbing it across my face, smacking it against my cheeks. I looked up at him and murmured, "You know just what I like."

"I have a feeling you like everything," he said.

We moved to the bed; Jake produced a condom, placing it on one of his nipples, where it looked sexier than any condom I'd ever seen. He told me to suck some more, which I gladly did. After a few minutes he lifted my head, slid the rubber over his cock, and raised me up, moving me around as effortlessly as if I was indeed a Barbie doll. I lowered my cunt onto his cock, not even noticing it wore latex, leaned forward and let my tits fall into his mouth. He moved his hips slowly, giving me most, but not quite all, of his hard meat.

"Fuck me hard," I begged.

"Don't worry, you'll get it hard," he said, still holding back. This was clearly a man who would fuck me at his own pace in his own time, and also a man I could trust to do it well.

"Tighten your muscles," he said, rolling me onto my back. "Squeeze my cock with your pussy." I squeezed as hard as I could, desperate to please him. He lifted my legs higher and pumped into me, his bulk and weight driving all resistance from my body.

"Is that enough cock for you?" I groaned.

"Loosen up now," he grunted. "Let it go. Take me home, baby." As if I'd been involved in a long arduous struggle, I gave up at last, gratefully surrendering body and soul, totally at his command. Jake drove deeper and deeper into me, finally shuddering as he came.

Since our encounter I've been in an absolute fever. I think that Jake is, as my horoscope put it, going to prove to be quite a challenge. It's a challenge that I'm definitely ready for.

A Closer Encounter

By Blake C. Aarens

She doesn't like to admit it, but Tasha is lost. It's been over an hour since she last saw another car. The only illumination is from her headlights, and even on high beam, visibility is poor. She's a little hungry. A little tired.

The road makes a hairpin turn and there it is. Not lights, not a town, but a wide-open vista point. She can see peak after peak, valley after valley, like the knuckles of interlaced fingers.

Tasha stops the car and gets out. She should be able to see a car coming. If there was a car coming.

There is no car coming.

Tasha stands on a steep ridge somewhere in the Rocky Mountains. She sucks in the thin, cold air. She strains her ears against the silence. She looks up, but heavy clouds blot out the stars.

It comes from below her. An enormous star ship. It rises up from the deep basin of the earth bathed in light. Scarlet . . . vermilion . . . canary . . . aqua . . . indigo . . . violet—a shimmering wave of colored light. Each color muting, then bleeding into the next.

And then the colors are not outside her, but on her, in her. Red at her feet; her belly the color of a navel orange; her breasts heavy with yellow; her heart, a green, pulsing thing beneath them; her blue, blue throat. An indigo eye cracks open in her forehead; the top of her skull explodes in deep purple. Again and again. In waves. Bright, brighter, brightest. An explosion of light behind her eyes.

Then darkness.

She is inside the colors now. Part of the wave. She is encased in a jewel, seeing the world through its facets. The subtle shifts of light are soothing after the roar of color that overwhelmed her. Tasha draws a deep breath of relief. Ease floods into her body. And then she is struck by the fact of her own nakedness. Her clothes were there a moment ago. Not taken off or melted away or torn. Just gone.

And then she sees it.

Many limbed. Twice as tall as Tasha's five foot eight. It is thick. Heavy, but graceful. Its many arms float slowly toward Tasha's body. Tasha trembles uncontrollably. The creature's arms seem to be filling the space, and sooner or later they will catch her.

They do. She is lifted from the ground and cradled. Limbs encircle her waist, raise her chin, cup the back of her head. Imprisonment and embrace at the same time. The creature surrounds Tasha's entire body, almost encasing her within it. Now it is the creature's turn to tremble. A continuous loop of pleasure passes between them. A soft tentacle presses her cheek. Another worms its way between her breasts. Tasha twists and moans in the creature's embrace. The creature echoes her sound. Echoes it and sends the moan back between Tasha's lips, down her throat, into her belly. The creature begins to stroke her. To press and probe at her body. It studies the curve of her bottom and the swell of her breasts.

The tentacle squirming between Tasha's breasts ends in a mouth. A tiny, perfect mouth. With pursed lips. And teeth. It wanders over Tasha's breasts, planting kisses that leave spots of heat all along her skin and make her breath come fast.

An infinite number of tentacles rove all over Tasha's body. Stroking, caressing, pinching. Nibbling. A tentacle of her own—of her wetness—trails down the inside of Tasha's thigh.

The tiny, perfect little mouth travels over the roll of her belly, and through the thick bush of her pubic hair, to lick and suck there. Drinking.

More tentacles join the little mouth, pressing inquisitively at

Tasha's groin, spreading her legs, raising her cradled feet in the air, parting of the outer lips of her pussy. At the first contact of that perfect little mouth on her clitoris, her head snaps back, and her eyes roll up into their sockets.

Oh, the sucking.

Limbs and tentacles caress Tasha. Through the thick corkscrews of her hair.

Across her mouth. Down the nape of her neck. All the way down her back. Between her buttocks. Pressing against the tight little hole there. A tongue thicker and more agile than Tasha's own fills her mouth until she's forced to breathe out of her nose. She knows what is coming.

Her breasts, first cupped and caressed, are now suckled and bitten by two more, perfect, little, mouths. Tentacles slither between her thighs, spreading her wetness between the two holes. Her body arches in the creature's embrace, she is in a rolling orgasm, explosions of light between her legs, between her breasts, between her eyes.

And then she is entered. The anal probe of so many UFO stories. But this probe is not cold and metallic, but warm, gnarled and fleshy, oozing a wetness of its own. Pulsing. Entering her where things have only exited. Stretching her open and then filling the space it makes for itself.

And all the tentacles on her pussy. They rub her clitoris. Her opening. One thick limb thumps against her swollen flesh down there, and then begins to press, and press, and press against her. Her inner lips are stretched thin by the width of it. Slippery with all the juice flowing from her body, the creature's thick limb slips inside, boring into the cave of her. Impaling Tasha. Embracing Tasha. Absorbing Tasha.

The rest area is deserted. The sign carved in native stone reads:

Mayflower, Colorado

Elevation: 4378

Population: 35

Tasha breathes. Her nipples are stiff and sore, they tent the fabric of her t-shirt. She can feel her pulse throbbing in her clitoris through her too-tight jeans. Her pussy and anus feel swollen and a little tender. Tasha takes a slow, deep breath. She starts the engine and turns on the heat. She grabs the blanket from the backseat and wraps it around her. She drives through Mayflower and on out the other end.

Subway

BY YOHANNON

Trying to get comfortable (an almost impossible task standing in a subway car), she felt the hairs on the back of her neck begin to rise. Living in a large city had given her a healthy sense of paranoia, but this was . . . different.

Looking over the crowd, trying to seem casual—there didn't seem to be an obvious source for the feeling. She was about ready to shrug it off when the train gave out one of those long, drawn-out squeals, and she fell backward into the lap of a young man sitting behind her.

At first apologetic, she felt a bit put off: Why hadn't he offered her a seat? But she quickly suppressed the feeling as a remnant of her small-town upbringing. Also, at her current weight (she seemed to gain another 20 pounds after moving out of her parents' incredibly strict clutches, giving her a well-rounded and curvy figure, if a trifle bottom heavy), she was certain that she could have injured the poor man.

The "poor man" in question seemed to be in good humor about having her in his lap, and was trying to help her up, when the lights went out.

The train had come to a stop between stations, the sudden darkness producing the usual babble, moans and groans from the passengers. The stranger's hands, currently holding her waist, seemed to pause. She could almost hear him pondering the situation, when a sudden jolt as the train tried to move forward again sent her sitting fully in his lap.

Even through the skirt she could feel his obvious excitement, which took her breath away. She hadn't been feeling very attractive of late, and this evidence of his lust left her confused and (to her own surprise) quite excited. His arms were now around her waist, no longer quick to assist her to her feet, and she found that the feeling of his strong legs under her rump caused her to moisten in ways that made her blush.

She placed her hands over his, and he started to move them away. She clutched them tighter, and pulled them around her, pulling them up slightly. Thus encouraged, he began to relax, rubbing his hands over her ample belly and just below her breasts. She felt herself responding to the thrill of the situation, suppressing the more "sensible" part of her brain that shrilled about how dangerous this was.

Over-ruling it, she took one of his hands and, very deliberately (and before she could chicken out) placed it on one full breast. The other hand she nudged downward, too frightened to go through with moving it to where she wanted it to go, secretly hoping he would get the hint.

He did, and his hand slowly stroked over her belly, her thigh, and cupped her mound through her skirt. When the hand moved away, she had to bite her tongue to keep from crying out "No!"—but soon it returned . . . under the skirt, hitching it up from behind. The feeling of his fingers on the back of her thigh was electric, and she felt herself spreading her legs as far as she dared without risking giving away her position to the other riders crowded about them.

Again she felt the hand move away for a moment, only this time she felt anticipation, wondering what would happen next. She felt him shift beneath her slightly, and then the heat of something firm and slightly moist sliding on her skin.

She almost froze then, realizing that he was rubbing his hard cock between her thighs. His hand returned, sliding to her dampened crotch, gently sliding past her panties. She closed her legs slightly in response, which excited him all the more.

He gently stroked her vaginal lips, working his way inside, where she was already almost dripping wet. When his fingers finally reached her throbbing clit, she had to bite her lip to keep from moaning aloud.

They developed a simple rhythm quickly, as she squeezed her soft fleshy thighs around his erection, he pumped in and out slightly, and his fingers circled her inner lips. She found herself caught between the wish that this could last for hours, and the fear that the lights would come on suddenly, revealing their indiscretion.

He must have thought the same thing, because he seemed to pick up the pace of her stimulation quickly, expertly bringing her to the point of orgasm. As she began to shudder, she felt him shooting over her thighs, which sent her over the edge almost instantly, leaving her melted over him, their heavy breathing masked by the muttering of the crowd.

They sat there for several moments, basking in the afterglow. Slowly, reluctantly, his hands began to withdraw, giving parts of her farewell strokes that demonstrated his appreciation for the contact. When he finally brought her to her feet (with a firm heave with both hands squeezing her ass) she found herself thankful for the support of the metal bar. Her knees felt rubbery as he smoothed her skirt back down, the trickle of his come still dripping down her legs.

Not a moment too soon, as it turned out. With another jolt, the train began moving, and the lights returned to a smattering of applause. She couldn't help but blush at the idea the applause was for their performance, though almost no one could have known what they were doing. At least, that was what she hoped.

Suddenly shy, she couldn't bring herself to turn around to face him. As the train pulled into the next stop and the mob seethed around her, she felt something pressed into her hand. Turning around, she saw that he was gone, probably onto the station platform.

She didn't look at the card until she departed the train herself at her stop. It was just a phone number: No name was given. She pondered over it long after the train left the station, until a big smile spread over her face.

The Fever

By Marilyn Jaye Lewis

In the darkness, the Best family estate seemed even more ominous and foreboding than it did by daylight. Adelaide Best crept quietly past the silent rooms where her husband's family slept.

"Addy," Darl had said, waking her from a sound sleep only moments before, "I think I've a fever. Go down to the kitchen for me and fetch me a glass of something cold to drink. Anything. I'm terribly thirsty."

Adelaide now made her way down the sweeping flight of stairs. Off the grand hallway on the ground floor, she felt her way along a dark, narrow corridor that led to the servants' area of the large, Victorian home. Down at the end of the corridor, Adelaide saw a light coming from the housemaid's sleeping quarters. And she heard voices raised, an argument of some sort.

Perturbed, Adelaide crept closer to the room without making a sound. One of the voices was without question the voice of Archibald Best, Darl's father. It grew increasingly clear to Adelaide, by the temper and tone of the two voices, that Mr. Best was reprimanding a remorseful housemaid for some inexcusable infraction of a house rule.

"But why at this hour?" Adelaide wondered. "And why be so harsh with her?"

Adelaide's ears pricked up when next she heard Mr. Best strike the housemaid, as if with an open hand, and then heard the housemaid cry out.

Adelaide moved quickly to the door that was open a mere

crack, her heart racing. With a slight maneuvering of her head, Adelaide got a wicked eyeful. It was nothing at all like what she'd been expecting to see.

The housemaid, Beatrice, a rather plump young woman, was on the narrow bed, stripped entirely of her nightclothes. Wantonly naked, she was leaning down on her elbows with her knees spread wide. Her ample breasts hung down freely and her rather large white bottom was arched up salaciously for Mr. Best's unhindered view.

Mr. Best was in an appalling state. His silk dressing gown hung open just enough to reveal his extremely thick, bulging member that he stroked vigorously with one hand, while with his other hand, he periodically administered a smart and resounding smack to the fleshy behind of the housemaid, along with a stern warning about how not to behave.

Judging by the way Beatrice whimpered and squirmed in delight with each well-aimed slap to her rump, it was clear that the housemaid, as much as Archibald Best, was deriving a great deal of unspeakable pleasure from this charade.

Adelaide wanted to look away, and yet she couldn't. Her eyes remained fixed on the sight beyond the crack in the door.

Then to Adelaide's astonishment, Mr. Best fell to his knees and buried his face between Beatrice's plump thighs and licked her private places aggressively, as if he meant to devour her. And Beatrice didn't protest. She only accommodated him by spreading her knees wider and arching her fat rear end up higher.

In her efforts to see it all, Adelaide's body was practically pressed flat against the opening of the door. She was breathing heavily through her mouth. Absently, she fondled her breasts through the layers of her nightclothes. Her nipples were tender and responsive, which only caused her to fondle them more intently.

Mr. Best stood then and mounted Beatrice from behind, inserting that thick, bulging tool of his easily into Beatrice's hole.

"What an accommodating girl she is," Adelaide thought agreeably, as her eyes greedily took in the sight of the pair humping in unbridled lust, grunting lewdly, behaving no better than a couple of coarse dogs.

Then to Adelaide's horror, it was clear that someone was coming toward her in the dark corridor. She moved quickly away from the spectacle in the doorway and headed in the direction of the kitchen.

But a large, masculine hand had her by the back of her neck.

"What a naughty little peeper you are, peeping into private bedrooms at night."

The voice sounded like Archibald Best's but Adelaide knew that it couldn't be possible. Mr. Best was hard at work, fornicating with Beatrice, the maid.

"You know what happens to peepers around here, Addy?"

It was Adelaide's husband. It was Darl.

"Darl, you frightened me!"

Darl clamped a hand over Adelaide's mouth and pushed her into the pantry with him, pulling the door closed behind him, locking them in together.

In the dark, he pulled her warm body up against his—impossibly close, her round ass snug against his aching cock.

Adelaide could easily feel her husband's firm erection pressing insistently against her bottom. He was just as stirred up as she was.

"You knew!" she whispered breathlessly. "You knew I would see that! You haven't a fever at all!"

"I do have a fever, but of a different sort. Do you know how long I've been tortured by those two? Every Tuesday night for three years, Addy. I've been watching that scene over and over again. It hardly ever varies." Then he whispered pleadingly, "Bend over for me, Addy. Lift your gown and bend over for me."

Adelaide wasn't sure what shameful thing this was leading to, but she timidly raised her robe and her nightdress, lifted them high, up to her waist. She felt safe in the darkness of the pantry. She bent over slightly for Darl, anxious about what might happen next but feeling aroused enough by the things she'd just seen to surrender to her husband's will.

Darl knew then that his wife was just as susceptible to the fever as he was. He fell to his knees in the dark and without hesitating, buried his face between her legs. He licked excitedly at the strange slippery folds of flesh, his nose filling with the scent of her arousal.

"Darl," Adelaide moaned, spreading her legs more for him, feeling her tender lips become engorged from the thorough lapping of his tongue. She wanted to feel more of it, as much as she could get. She bent over farther for him, arching her ass out.

"Oh Darl," she moaned again, over and over, not caring if she was overheard. "Darl, Darl," she said, oblivious to the obscene posture she was taking in the dark, wanting only to feel more pleasure from his tongue.

Next he stood and mounted her—from behind, like a dog. And she didn't say no, for once. She didn't protest. She accepted the full length of his thick erection repeatedly, pushing her hole open for his merciless thrusts, letting his cock go all the way up.

Quietly Adelaide urged him on, "Yes, yes," as if she were in a daze, succumbing deeper to the fever of her husband's lust with every plunge of his relentless cock.

And Darl knew then that it was a question of persistence. He was going to be able to have his wife in any position he desired, even with the lamp burning, so that he might see her secret places, watch the tiny hole stretch to accommodate the girth of his impaling cock. Then the fever of Beatrice would no longer torment him. He would abstain from the salacious sight of her for good. It would be just him and Addy, from this moment on.

All Eyes On Her

By M. Christian

The city sat around her. From where she was standing, nothing but the silver squares of windows seemed to be watching. But she knew better; she could feel them sitting behind their desks, in their living rooms, in the bedrooms, in their beds, watching her.

The gravel and tarpaper of the roof was hot underfoot, but she enjoyed it. It was the totality of it, the completeness of the act, that made her nipples into hard knots, and stoked the fire of her cunt. Wearing slippers, shoes, or anything else would've made it incomplete, would've ruined the statement: standing naked on the rooftop, letting the city watch her.

At first Cindy didn't think she could do it. It was a private thing, a crazy thing, something to lay back in a warm, soapy tub and think about—rubbing herself into a rolling orgasm. In the real world the roof was hot, the gravel hurt the bottoms of her feet, and a hard, chill wind cut over the concrete edge of the roof and blasted through her.

Despite the pains in her feet, the chill air, and the hot tar, she stood naked on the roof of her little five-story apartment building, a fire roaring in her cunt.

— *there, that little square: formed out of un-athletic dough, he watched her. His cock was small, and barely hard. He pulled it, tugged at it, the warm roll of his stomach brushing his hand as he masturbated. Slowly, he got harder and harder till all of his few inches was strong and hard in his hand. The fat man watched, smiling, happy and excited. When he came, he selflessly groaned, and got his window messy.*

Cindy watched the city watching her. Looking at one silvery window in particular she lifted her right hand to her left breast and stroked the soft skin and pinched the hard nipple.

—*they watched her. Taken with her brazenness, the attitude of this obvious species of urban nymph, who could say who started it? Maybe it was Mike who first dropped his shorts and started the kiss, his rock-hard cock fitting so perfectly, so nicely between them. But then it could've been Steve who started it, who put his hand between them to feel his own straining erection. Was it Mike who dropped to his knees and started a grand suck? Or was it Steve? Who came first? Did Steve fill Mike's mouth with bittersweet come? Or did Mike explode all over Steve's face? Or did it really matter? The end certainly justified the means . . .*

Cindy looked up at the sun. It bathed her, baked her; her skin vibrated with the heat of it, the fire it coated her with. Right still on left, she felt her breast, playing with the texture of it, the under-lying muscle, the strong tip of her nipple. Sun on her, she moved left to right, massaging her breasts under the gaze of the warm sun.

— *sitting on their bed, she watched the woman on the rooftop across the street. The sun was almost too bright, too hot, and for a moment she thought about what she had to do: shower, get dressed, go to work. But the woman, the daringness of her, the casualness of her, kept her glued to the window. She didn't seem crazy, but that's what she had to be. To stand up there in the sight of God and everyone else, and rub herself like that. It turned her on something fierce. It made her horny, that's what it did. She savored the word as she pulled herself up from sitting to all fours. Her breasts pulled away from her body in this position — they strained against her body and rolled in her housedress. Without thinking, she put a hand down the front of her dress and cradled one of her breasts. The nipple was so hard it ached, it was so hard. Cautiously, she squeezed and pulled gen-tly at it. Fire raced through her. Her legs felt like they were going to collapse. The woman across the street, touching herself, it was like she was crazy, touching herself and thinking about her nipples and between her legs she could feel herself grow wet —*

Her legs were tired, so Cindy lowered herself down till she squatted over the hot gravel roof. Her breasts were heavy and tight, her nipples ached to be touched and sucked. No thought. Not a one. Watching the city watching her, Cindy put a hot hand between her hot legs. Her thighs were wet, her cunt was a damp forest of blond curls. Her lips were wet and hot. She ran a single finger from her clit to her cunt to her ass, and shivered in delight.

— bent over the chair, her ass in the air, her arms down the chair back, her knees on the seat, Betty could feel Bob's tongue playing with her cunt. He loved to eat her, and, God, he was good at it. She pushed herself back towards his face, trying to get his hard, strong, tongue deeper into her soaking cunt. Then he found her puckered asshole, and started to tongue around it. Christ! She felt like screaming. She needed cock now, right now in her soaking pussy, she needed to be filled, fucked, she wanted to come and come and come! Then Bob was at her clit, and the world seemed to boil down to the points of her nipples, the glow of her ass, the wetness of her cunt, her lover's tongue, and the joy of her clit. She was so lost, so incredibly lost getting ready to come, that she almost forgot to look up, to look across the way to see what that chick on the roof was doing next —

Cindy's cunt juice ran between her fingers. She was so wet. Her cunt was soaking, her clit was a hard bead between her legs, tucked between her lips. She'd worked out a system, and it was working real good: first she'd plunge her hands deep within herself, up and deep till she could swear there was her cervix, there her G-spot. Then she'd pull out, slow and hard, pushing aside her hot, soaking lips till her fingers glided past her clit. Then she'd work it, rubbing around and around the little bead of her clit. Then back—back to her cunt, the depths of her, her hot lips, her clit, over and over again.

Sometimes she'd use both hands, pushing all fingers into herself like some huge cock. Sometimes she'd use just one, saving the other, wet and smelling of her cunt, on the knots of her nipples, her aching breasts.

Then she came, fast and oh-so-hard, with the whole world watching.

Under the Camel Light

By Muzelle

At the ripe age of 19, I landed a solo pad halfway up the west-side slope of Nob Hill. The original renter skipped off to Europe for the year, so my sublease rate was to die for and the place was fully furnished. Unmistakably, it was the sweetest, most charming studio in the whole city. Of course, I couldn't help but adore it because it was my first. Hardwood floors, old claw-foot tub, checker-board kitchen tiles . . . and a squeaky old Murphy bed to boot. The view, however, left much to be desired.

My one and only window was directly aligned with another Edwardian complex. So nothing but a six-foot gap and an old rusty fire escape inhibited the Smiths and Joneses from sharing my quarters. Most of the tenants kept to themselves, though, so I figured they might as well have been living in Zimbabwe. Aside from Pete, that is.

Pete was a chain smoker. And Big Brains lived with a cat that was allergic to nicotine. Ergo, the fire escape became his second home. If my window was open, a fresh breeze chocked full o' Camel Light incense never failed. I began to hate cigarettes with a passion—despite my addiction to bumming them from friends.

I seriously contemplated offering to swap cats with Pete just to get him off the fire escape. But since our first "How do?" we never talked. And I sure as hell wasn't going to lose the silent game. Besides, my little fur ball was positively more precious than his.

As it turned out, Pete was never a bother. He never spoke. I sup-pose he was trying to be as considerate of my privacy as possible. So I made up my mind to pretend he lived in Zimbabwe with everyone else in that building.

But I will never forget the last night of my first month at that place. I had gone to Baker Beach with Johnny, an incredibly hot, adoringly witty old sex buddy. We bared it all under the hot sun.

"I heard you really have to protect against penile burn on these nudie beaches," I hinted. Johnny smirked and was oh-so-kind as to let me rub liberal amounts of sunscreen onto his anxious, uncut cock.

In return, he read the dirty bits of a nasty novel to me as he lightly tracked my treasure trail with his finger. Intermittently, when our fair fellow beachers looked away, he teased my anxious, throbbing clit. First a couple of light taps . . . then a few soft ringlets . . . and ultimately a machine gun finale.

My tail wagging, I asked, "Hey, wanna skip the sunset and head back?" As if I had to twist his prick. By no shock, I couldn't wait to dash home and jump his bones, and he had no qualms. So we scurried back to my digs.

He heated the shower while I pulled down the Murphy, lit my candles and turned on the soft purrs of France Gall (60s-famed, French sex kitten extraordinaire). "Showtime," I thought to myself.

Entering the steamy bathroom, I peeled open the curtain and slowly gyrated my pelvis for Johnny as I lowered my bikini to my thighs. Beads of sand gently scraped my skin as I ran my hands over my freed breasts and down my heated, damp bodice.

Pulling Johnny's shampooed head near, I gave him a deep, lustful kiss and gathered a handful of suds for play. Lifting a leg and tracing it in bubbles, then rubbing them over my hips and belly, I danced slowly and my wide eyes coyly stared back at him.

Eye candy he couldn't resist. He stroked his cock and watched eagerly.

With one arm outstretched on the wall to support me, I straddled my legs, arched my back and heavily coated my ass with glimmering white suds. Then playfully slapping my wet flesh, I spanked myself until it hurt and intermittently petted away the sting.

"Get in here, pleeeaasse," he begged.

"Why? I'm having so much fun out here." The waiting game. Hard-earned wisdom reminded me that frequent acts of immediate gratification create ungrateful lovers. Moreover, the sight of him panting and salivating was too endearing to sacrifice.

He wrapped his arms around my waist and reached down to fondle my clit, pulling me toward the shower. Turning me around he grabbed my hair with one hand, clenched my ass with the other and began to bite my nipples mercilessly.

"Aaiii ... Revenge!" I thought. Just the type I liked. I jumped in the shower and in no time his hard, throbbing sex penetrated my wet, ravenous pussy.

Johnny was a vigorous screw. Notably the only man I'd ever met who could nearly outdo me in marathon sex. Yes, he was a fucking machine. And he liked to play. He could return any ball I served him.

His half-tempered cock still inside me, we crab-walked our way to the bed and rang the bell for round two.

I joked, "You're almost as good as the lover I had this morning." I spanked his bright pink ass hard and told him to ride me and fuck me like the whore I am. Ask and you shall receive.

This boy knew how to move. He was fucking me hard and fast when he grabbed a handful of my hair, yanked my head to the side and whispered into my ear, "Yeah that's right . . . you are a dirty slut . . . aren't you? . . . Yep . . . you're my little fuck-hole . . . that's right." He not only fucked like a pro, but he could talk dirty like a porn star, too.

As Johnny continued to call me his bitch, slut, whore . . . you name it . . . I smelt something remarkably familiar. And it certainly wasn't Johnny's cologne. Nor was it the smell of Johnny's cum. No, this scent was not nearly that enticing.

Sure enough, I opened my eyes and saw Pete on the fire escape, smoking his Camel Light. He was leaning back on the black metal rail and staring right at me. Eye-to-eye.

Shell-shocked, I thought, "So much for being considerate of my privacy." But in an instant I felt more perplexed than offended. My mind told me I should be feeling outraged, humiliated and violated . . . but my body was screaming something else!

Somehow the way he looked intently into my eyes, the way he didn't flinch when I caught him looking and the way Johnny continued fucking me as if it were just he and I were all strangely and powerfully erotic to me. What is more, I couldn't take my eyes off Pete. And I came, immediately, like floodwaters breaking down a dam.

Johnny was going strong and wasn't about to stop. My praise for his staying power always motivated him to record extremes. And Pete's eyes told me he wasn't going anywhere, either. Our eyes remained fixated as my third orgasmic wave series came rushing in. Pete lit up his third cigarette.

So Johnny and I fucked, sucked, spanked, licked, whipped, kissed, cradled and caressed one another until sunrise. We even brought out our latex playwear. And Pete was there, watching and smoking, all night long.

Johnny never admitted to seeing anyone in the darkness. But my hunch is that Johnny knew we were under the spotlight. I swear he performed like he never had before.

For me, that night was just the beginning. From then on, whenever I fucked in that studio Pete was there. He never skipped a beat. His piercing, magical eyes catapulted my orgasms into a sublime realm . . . every time. In total, 372 times . . . but who's counting?

Since then I've moved to a new place with much less vigilant neighbors—despite my efforts to gain their attention. Dining naked . . . washing windows in red-lace panties... hell, even vocal sex with a mini-microphone. Nothing seems to interest the dullards. No matter. Pete is imprinted into my mind's eye forever: His eyes gazing intently into mine with a Camel Light dangling from his quiet, sheepish grin.

Disco Nap

BY CHARLIE ANDERS

*P*arty girls learn the routine after college, when the prospect of twenty hours' wakefulness at a stretch seems less and less practical. Come home from work Friday evening, eat a light supper and maybe sip some spritzer, then retire to bed for a couple of hours. Emerge at ten, just when the clubs are getting worth visiting. My "disco naps" usually included a facial, followed by an eye mask and enough moisturizer to rehydrate the Sahara. Put Enya on the stereo, burn some incense and clear your mind for the long night among the upwardly, downwardly, horizontally and gyrationally mobile.

And then I got together with Ray, who hated naps. And discos. He wouldn't go clubbing unless it was a five-day weekend and someone's birthday. I had met Ray at a club, so I felt false advertising was at work here.

"I just want to stay in and watch a video," he keened. When he started in on that shit, I just made drum machine noises with my mouth until he stopped. "Bfft—ssst—bfft—ssst," four on the floor, techno-style, the unbreakable chain of beats. He gave up and pretended to dance to my oral rhythm track. He ground his hips against mine, a sly look on his heart-shaped face. O.K., so he did have some good points despite the homebody thing—a gymnast's body and blue eyes.

I stopped beat-boxing but he didn't stop jutting his pelvis into mine, to the four-four meat grinder mix.

"O.k., cut it out. I gotta crash if I'm going to be up in time to hit 26 Mix by ten—" I pulled off my jacket and blouse and tossed them on a chair.

"Mmm, bedtime?" Ray inquired, still that crafty aspect on his face.

"Not that kind of bedtime." I pulled off my wool skirt and slid off my nylons. Lit incense, turned off but one small light.

"Romantic," Ray said.

I crawled onto the bed. "Sleep now."

"Let me just massage your feet. You're going to be doing all that dancing."

Party girls never turn down a foot rub. And Ray was good. So I let him lift my left foot and run his hands over it. "Oooh," I breathed. His touch sent sparks all over my body—to my belly, my breasts and even my scalp. I shifted to bring my foot a little closer to him.

"Just think, soon this poor foot will find itself strapped into a narrow shoe with a cruel pointy toe and a spiky heel that will force pressure into your poor arch and toes," Ray whispered. "What a misfortune to befall such a beautiful, sensitive foot."

"Forget it," I breathed, half awake. "You can't sway me."

He kept finding pressure points that poured warmth into all of my tired muscles. And his hands also caused a stirring somewhere else. I let out a little purring sound and twisted my body.

"Don't worry," he whispered. "I'm not going to try and talk you out of your plans. You should put on your sexiest little outfit and your hottest heels and get out there and strut your stuff. Everyone at the club needs to see you decked out like a star, a shimmering doll with porcelain skin that everybody just wishes they could taste. You can't possibly deprive all those clubgoers of the fantasy of their tongues caressing that spot behind your kneecaps and that little area one inch below your belly button. All those party people with their tongues just twitching to make contact with your inner ankle, just for a second. You can't possibly rob the club of your hip-shaking sexual rabble rousing, can you?"

I shook my head. And my hips. I moved my body as if practicing for the club. Ray kept rubbing my foot, but one hand moved up and petted my ankle. Fingers fluttered over that little knob that sticks out over my instep, then the sensitive seam above that.

I still had my eyes closed. But I wasn't even trying to sleep. Ray put his perfect smooth mouth around my big toe and used his tongue and teeth to surround it with sensation. I shivered. He licked in between my toes and along the side of my left foot, massaging my right foot all the while.

"It's not going to work," I mutter.

"What isn't? I'm helping you prepare for your night out." I felt tingly and barely aware I was twisting this way and that on my bed. Ray pressed on my instep and tickled my calf at the same time. I scrunched down to give him access to my inner thighs, which he took. Both hands played along the skin from my kneecaps to my pelvis, making me giggle and beg. Then Ray moved his head between my legs and nuzzled. He did this for a while. I stopped pretending to nap.

Talking wasn't the only thing Ray knew how to do with that big mouth. Thank goodness. I grabbed two handfuls of sheet and arched my back. His tongue circled, then flicked, then circled again. I almost started to cry.

Then Ray came face to face with me and kissed me. I bit his neck. He slid on a condom, then ground against me, teasing me with his stiffness. Ray wasn't much taller or heavier than me, but when he got on top of me he managed to surround and encompass me. It was like I was inside him instead of vice versa. His arms and thighs covered me with frenetic muscles, and his face brushed mine. I saw dandelions bloom in his eyes just before my pubic bone thrust into his and I felt energy flood my body from the middle outward, almost more than I could stand.

Afterwards, we lay and did the afterglow thing. "So," Ray said after a few moments in my arms. "Wanna watch a video and cuddle?"

I broke out of his embrace and headed for the bathroom. "Nah. That was a great nap substitute, thanks. And I still have plenty of time to hook up with the crew at 26 Mix if I start my beauty routine now." I pushed my face into the bathroom sink with the water running, to drown out Ray's mock cry of anguish at his foiled scheme. Serves him right for trying to keep a party girl down.

Give Me a Shine

By Melanie Votaw

Shiny black shoes. Bright, glistening, freshly polished boots. These had always been among her favorite things. When she was a little girl, she loved to watch her father get his shoes shined. That fascination stayed with her to adulthood, as she still loved the smell of the polish, the men reading their papers, and the shoeshine guys buffing with old worn-out rags.

She had recently dispensed with her pumps and decided to wear only boots—short ones, tall ones, black ones, brown ones, white ones—but only boots that needed to be shined on a regular basis. She loved to sit high above the shoeshine guy and feel him inadvertently massage her feet through the leather.

One day she arrived for her normal shine, but the face that looked up and smiled at her as he placed her shoes on the metal platforms was a new face. Boyish, but strong, he gazed at her with enormous blue eyes and spoke with an accent she could not quite place. "These are very nice boots."

"Thank you," she responded, studying him. "You're new. Where are you from?"

"Brazil. I am just here and wanting to go to university, but my English needs get better," he said slowly, trying to choose the correct words.

"Your English is very good." He just smiled and continued stroking her boots with brush and rag. His hands were large with long fingers. His sun-streaked brown bangs fell onto his forehead and bounced as he leaned down between her knees to spray the leather with a water bottle.

"He can't be more than 18," she thought to herself, drinking in his sweet face and strong forearms. She moaned audibly when his work reached a particularly needful part of her tired feet. He looked up and appeared startled. "Oh, it just always feels a bit like a foot massage," she said, embarrassed. He gave her a flirtatious grin and continued. "I guess," she chuckled to herself, "their mostly male clientele is careful not to moan no matter how good it feels."

Next time she went for a shine, she asked for this same boy. She found out more and more about him, including that his name was Marcelo, that he was 19 years old and wanted to study veterinary medicine. She enjoyed his polite but flirty personality. As the weeks passed, her visits became more frequent and their conversations more personal and teasing. She felt certain he wanted her, but she hesitated. After all, she was 25. "Well, it's not like I'm an old lady, and it's not like he's illegal," she told herself.

One day, as she passed a shoe store, she saw the sexiest pair of stiletto boots in the window. They were red and sleek and tall. Even though they were quite expensive, she knew she had to have them. She also knew she wanted Marcelo to shine them as soon as possible. For that, she needed to make them appear used. Laughing at herself, she took them from their box and walked outside, adding a few scuffs and brushing some mud onto them.

She was always careful to wear slacks when she got a shoeshine, but the next day, she wore a tight dress with a short skirt. She knew he would be able to see her panties when he pulled her feet apart to place them on the metal foot supports. Luckily, her chair faced a wall, so only Marcelo could see what she chose to reveal.

He seemed stunned when he had to place her feet on the supports, as if he was somehow supposed to do so without exposing her. She pretended as if she had no idea there was a problem, and he placed her feet there, trying hard not to stare between her legs.

Wanting to leave a little to the imagination, she wore pink panties that were brief but opaque. They continued to talk as normally as possible, but his eyes kept returning to her crotch, only to dart quickly back to her feet.

"Obviously, he's afraid to make a move," she thought. "I guess I'll have to do it." Next day, she wore a different pair of boots and an even shorter skirt. She passed by the shoeshine place during her lunch break to find him busy. She asked when he would have time to give her a shine, and he pulled her to him, whispering, "Come back at 6:30."

She knew the business closed at 6:00, so perhaps he was ready for action after all! The hours and minutes ticked by at a snail's pace, but just before leaving her office, she retired to the ladies' room and removed her panties.

Marcelo had been trusted to close up shop and was the only one there when she arrived at 6:30 on the dot. He gestured her toward the chair, locked the door, and closed the blinds. She held her legs together and down between the foot supports. When he lifted her left foot, his eyes bulged. He brought her other foot to the platform and, this time, gazed openly between her legs. He bent down and lifted her feet onto his shoulders, kissing the right boot from the ankle to the knee. Then, he drew her knees over his shoulders, as his mouth moved magnetically toward her aching flesh.

She could feel his mouth tremble slightly as it closed over her labia, kissing her at first the way he would begin kissing her mouth. "We have never even kissed," she thought, as his tongue swept up and down. "Well, I guess this counts," she sighed and slumped farther down in the chair.

What he lacked in skill, he made up for with enthusiasm. His tongue slid and flicked and circled everywhere on her swollen pussy. When he started to suck her clit, she thought she would fall over the edge, but the last thing she wanted to do was rush. He certainly showed no signs of tiring, as he slurped ravenously, drinking her juices, and probing her depths with his long tongue. When she started to hump uncontrollably toward his face, he slid his hands under her hips to support her.

Just as her orgasm began to take her over, he inserted a finger inside her, and she pumped her hips forcefully upward against him with every delicious contraction. She wondered if anyone walking by could hear their cries. He moaned loudly too, as he simultaneously came in his pants.

"Oh, no, you made a mess!" she said, pointing at his crotch.

"It's okay. I have clothes in the back."

He lifted her up, holding her by her ass, and kissed her deeply. She wrapped her legs around his waist, and he carried her into the back room, where they finished giving each other a very good shine.

Kinsey Six

BY THOMAS S. ROCHE

When I get home, I almost turn around and walk out. I can hear you moaning. It's almost two in the morning; you said it was fine if I came home by midnight, so I'm pissed. The bedroom door is wide open. I can hear the two of you moaning, and I've got a straight line of sight into the bed, where you're spread open and she's between your thighs, eating you out.

We discussed this. We decided it was important to you to keep this partner, to remain lovers with her even though you and I had made a commitment. It's called poly-fucking-amory, and the most important thing about it is that we keep our agreements, isn't it? The fact that I've come home two hours after you said it was okay, and you're still fucking like bunnies with the bedroom door open, makes a surge of rage go through me.

But I watch. I don't turn around and walk out, because it's so damn late and I don't want to go get a motel or kill time at the 24-hour diner.

And besides, I've never seen Cora naked before.

She's sprawled out on the bed, hanging over the edge as she eats you out. Her nude body is slender, even skinny, but her hips have just enough swell to make my eyes linger there. She's got a tattoo of two female symbols intertwined on her lush ass. Her legs are spread and I can see her pussy, shaved and pierced.

Your eyes open and you see me in the doorway. You smile.

Shameless. You're fucking looking at me and not even caring that you've broken your agreement with me, that you and Cora are still fucking when I walk in the door. But you don't stop, you don't ask

Cora to stop. Instead, you blow me a kiss.

Then Cora lifts her head from your pussy and turns to look over her shoulder, her face glistening in the flicker of candlelight. You always light candles when you fuck.

Cora smiles.

"Hi, Mike," she says, and winks at me.

Then she goes back to eating your pussy.

Watching you, I feel my cock stirring in my pants. You've locked eyes with me and I can't look away. Your lips part and you start moaning again as Cora returns to tonguing your clit. You've described that technique to me many times, told me how she does it, but I've never quite been able to get it perfect. Cora has got it perfect. I can tell you're going to come.

I think back on the conversation we had where we negotiated this. "We'll be done by midnight, and she'll sleep on the couch," you said. "I promise, you won't have to see anything."

"It's all right if you're not done by midnight," I said. "Just make sure you close the bedroom door."

You smiled, kissed me on the forehead. "Oh, we'll close the bedroom door," you told me. Then, with a wicked smile, you added: "Unless we want you to join in."

At the time, I'd blown it off, thinking from the girlish giggle you gave that you were just teasing me. After all, Cora's a lesbian, isn't she? A dyed-in-the-wool femme Kinsey six, you told me. I ignored it.

But after all, a deal is a deal.

We should negotiate this, shouldn't we? Fuck it. The die is cast.

I take my clothes off. You watch me as I do, never offering a protest, just moaning in time with Cora's tongue on your clit. Cora doesn't even look up until I'm already naked, until my cock is standing out straight and hard and I'm next to the bed, watching from an improved vantage point as her face works up and down between your thighs. That's when she looks up at me and smiles.

"Oooh," she said. "I thought you'd never ask."

She reaches up and grabs my cock, pulling me down onto the bed. Her mouth, the mouth that's moved so skillfully on your clit, closes over my cock and she swallows it down, her lips working up and down on my shaft as I look down into her pretty face. She's got her eyes upturned toward me, and in the candlelight I can see the shimmer inside them. You lean forward and wrap your fingers around the base of my cock, feeling Cora's lips linger halfway down my shaft.

"Cora hasn't sucked cock in ten years," you say. "Don't you feel honored?"

"Hell, yes," I say, as your face burrows under Cora's and you begin to kiss my balls. I kneel there on the bed not knowing what to do, but Cora's sprawled out under me with her gorgeous ass looking delectable, and her legs are spread wide. I'm enough taller than her that I can lean over and reach between them.

When I touch her pussy I feel how incredibly wet it is. Her whole body stiffens, and for a moment I think I've gone too far. Then she moans rapturously, the vibrations traveling through my hard cock and into my body, and she starts to suck my cock in earnest as I finger her pussy.

You kneel on the bed and kiss me, your tongue lazing into my mouth as you run your fingers through my hair. "She wants you to fuck her," you whisper. "She's been talking about it all night."

"I thought she was a Kinsey six," I hiss.

"Haven't you heard?" you whisper. "There's a new scale. She's right in the middle."

Then you lean down close to her and say, "Mike's going to fuck you now, Cora."

You guide me around behind her, and I slide easily between her spread thighs. The rings of her lips prickle my shaft as I slide into her. She gasps, her pussy tight as it embraces me. You position yourself at her face, spreading your legs so she can eat you as I fuck her from behind. Her hand goes underneath her and she starts to work her own clit. I fuck her slowly at first, picking up speed as she begs "Harder," her fingers moving faster on her clit as she urges me on. Then I feel her pussy clenching around my shaft as she moans into your cunt, and that's all it takes to send me over the edge. As she finishes coming, I let myself go inside her, filling her with my come.

The three of us crawl up on the bed, and Cora and I start kissing while you cuddle up next to us and watch, lazily stroking your cunt. I can taste your pussy on her mouth.

"I guess you're not a six any more," I say.

"Let's call it five point five," she whispers, and curves her fingers around my soft cock, slick with her juices. You kiss my ear, your tongue warm.

The Real Reason I Have Long Hair

By Rachel Kramer Bussel

My grandmother wants me to cut my hair. I don't want to. I can't tell her why, but I can tell you.

It all started after a night out with a friend. We were sitting in her car after she'd driven me home. I'd called the friend I was staying with minutes earlier to let her know that I'd be home soon. I leaned over to give her a hug and thank her for the evening, and in a split-second the entire tenor of the evening changed. It went from an innocent hug to a goodnight kiss, and then it happened: she pulled my hair. And she didn't pull it lightly, by the split ends, the kind of tug a 6-year-old uses to tease the girl sitting next to him. No, it wasn't like that at all. It wasn't like anything I'd ever experienced before. She grabbed my hair by its roots near the back of my neck, and, using a surprising amount of force, tugged me by the hair. I felt that pull run right through my body and my cunt tightened. With each pull, I felt almost like I was getting fucked, or teased, the way the intensity built up and up until I could hardly breathe. It was a magical, thrilling moment that not only caught me off guard but also got me as aroused as I've ever been.

Having long hair has always been a sensual experience for me. When I'm naked after a shower and my hair has just dried, I love to lean back as far as I can and feel my hair caress my back like a lover, brushing against the curves of my ass. I love to tease my lovers with my hair, flicking it back and forth as I flirt, dangling it over their skin while we make love. I can use my long hair to flirt with, or to hide behind. It's also a bit of a camouflage; some people make assumptions that girls with long hair are "nice" and we're not supposed to be as brazen as girls who've chopped all their locks off. Long hair is supposed to be a bit dowdy, a bit old-fashioned, but for me it's not; it's intimately connected to my sexuality. And in many ways my actions are like a girl with short hair; I'm very independent, headstrong, outspoken. But there is a totally girlish side of me, one that delights in something as seemingly retro as long hair.

Every time it's too hot out or my hair gets too frizzy, I have the urge to take a pair of scissors and chop it off, lose the split ends and extra care long hair requires, maybe cooler, or dykier, in the process. But always, always, I resist. Long hair makes me feel powerful, sexy, beautiful, and every time I've cut it off, I've missed it desperately.

In a total act of topping from the bottom, I often command my lovers to pull my hair, hard. When they do, it sends shivers throughout my body, a current of energy channeling from the roots of my hair directly to my cunt. I get frenzied and frantic as they pull over and over, each tug building on the next. It's like being teased, touched lightly or indirectly when you just want to be pounded hard. Because while having my hair pulled can bring me right up to the brink of orgasm, it alone is not enough, and that maddening tease, that thrill as the sensations chase me closer and closer, is like nothing else.

When I'm having an intense hair pulling session, I lose myself completely, get frantic and needy and one hundred percent out of control. I want things I've never wanted before when my hair is being pulled, things that scare me and test my boundaries. Tears spring to my eyes, but they're not from a direct sense of pain, because it doesn't hurt, at least not in the way I understand pain. When a lover pulls my hair just right, with that perfect combination of domination and affection, my head bends back in pure submission and delight. Parts of me I don't usually think of as erogenous zones come to life. The girl who pulled my hair and almost made me come under the street lamp also pinched my neck (something nobody had ever done before), precisely and deliberately coinciding with her hair pulling, sending further spasms throughout my splayed-out body.

On vacation with my lover, he was pulling my hair as I straddled him, our bodies rubbing together, and all of a sudden, I wanted him to slap me, hard, across the face. I'd never wanted that or anything like it before, and the thought and image scared me even as they turned me on. I opened my mouth but couldn't get any words out, couldn't voice this seemingly wrong desire. So he kept pulling my hair and biting my nipples, working me into such a frenzy I thought I would explode. I knew that all of this pain-as-pleasure stuff was new to him, but it was also new to me, in a way; I didn't expect his hair pulling to have such an effect. It can totally make me lose my balance, both mental and physical, spin me and twist me around so I hardly know where I am or what I want. That kind of dizzying desire is scary, but also special (perhaps because it's so scary).

It's also a special kind of activity, not something I do with every lover. That very first night, what made it so special was the surprise element, the way I didn't know what would come next or where she would take me. What makes me keep wanting more and more is that I still don't know what will come next—what bizarre thoughts and fantasies will enter my mind and body when someone pulls my hair.

So now you know my secret, the reason I put up with the knots and tangles and hassles of having hair halfway down my back. It's not just a fashion statement; it's a sexual proclamation for those who are bold enough to handle it. Just don't tell my grandmother.

Gwen Is Wet

By David Henry Sterry

First day of soccer practice, and someone's staring. When Gwen turned around and caught him, he didn't look away. His eyes are so deep and blue, Gwen thought, as she dove into them. He was almost smiling. Like he wanted something from her. When Gwen closed her eyes to go to sleep that night she saw that look. Hungry. Blue.

He was the new coach. 20-ish. Even when he was standing still, the muscles in his thighs looked like cinder blocks. Gwen caught herself staring. He wore paper-thin t-shirts from Brazil, Ireland, Germany, Mozambique, Mazatlan. Where he'd been. Kissing beautiful exotic women, Gwen caught herself imagining. She'd only had one boyfriend, and when he kissed her, he jammed his mouth onto hers hard. So she broke up with him. New Coach had curly brown hair and a crooked nose from when it was broken. A scar over one of his blue eyes. Where did that scar come from? Gwen wondered.

Gwen stared at her naked body in the mirror in her girly room. Whose breasts are those? They looked beautiful to her, like a painting in a museum. But they didn't seem like hers. That strange new fullness between her legs. She felt as if she had a new Christmas present, but someone had forgotten to tell her how it works.

New Coach was coming over. Gwen still couldn't believe she'd gotten up the nerve to ask him. She hadn't told any of her friends. Which was odd, because Gwen told her friends everything. That made Gwen nervous. And her parents were gone for the weekend. Gone, gone, gone. That made Gwen very nervous.

Gwen opened the front door, and the New Coach was standing

there. Almost smiling. Hungry. Blue. In a paper-thin faded t-shirt from Monte Carlo with red shorts over his large brown legs.

Then they were sitting on the couch. Talking.

"So, where are your parents?" he asked.

"Oh, they're away for the weekend," Gwen said, with an air of casual offhandedness that didn't fool anyone.

"Really . . . " he said, almost smiling.

My God, those eyes are blue, Gwen found herself thinking.

"So, where do you wanna watch the video?" Gwen asked.

"Anywhere," said the New Coach.

"How about up in my room?" slipped out of her, and once it was out, there was no taking it back.

"Sure," he almost smiled.

Something inside Gwen heated up, stole her breath, made her blood flow.

He's sitting next to Gwen on her bed, watching his soccer video. Goal after goal crashed into nets. Men hugging. Kissing. Crowd going crazy. His thick brown leg was so close she could feel the heat coming off it. The longer Gwen sat there not watching goal after goal being rammed home, the more confused Gwen became. Why is he just sitting there?

Finally Gwen realized: I'm the one that's hungry. Is he hungry, too?

"Goooooooooooooooooooooooooooooaaaalll!" erupted every thirty seconds on the soundtrack. He's not going to do anything. He can't. It would be creepy if he did. It's my move, Gwen, thought. My move.

"I've . . . been having, uh . . . problems with my back, and I was wondering . . . if you could . . . stretch me?" she asked.

"Sure," he almost smiled.

She was on her back. He was standing over her. He bent down and put his huge hands on her legs, freshly shaved, and he was staring into her so blue, his voice soft, hypnotic and hungry:

"Breathe."

She breathed.

"Deep," he said. "Let it go, Gwen."

How am I supposed to let it go, Gwen thought, when I don't even know what it is?

He pulled her right knee up into her chest, then moved her right knee across her body, stretching her torso, his huge hand spreading strong across the outside of her thigh, the other above her breast.

"Breathe . . . " he said, "deep."

She breathed. Deep.

He stretched her, deep into her big muscles, all the way inside her, whoosh, a deep spinal relief, the tight unloosening with every breath. Gently he pushed while she breathed, one huge hand drifting onto her pelvis over her white underpants.

Gwen is wet.

She wants to give him something. She wants to get something from him.

Gwen saw it outlined against his thin red shorts. Hard. Then his enormous thumb was pressing firm gentle and hungry, fitting perfectly against her, and Gwen felt herself stick to her white underpants, hotly and wetly, pressing into his thumb, and she sighed hard, shivered and shook.

She smelled him. Smelled her. Smelled sex.

She felt him through his thin red shorts. Moved him so instead of his thumb pressing against her, she felt him pressing against her, sliding along her wet with the rhythm of their breath.

"Breathe, Gwen," he whispered in her ear, laid his chest on her chest, bodies melting into each other.

She breathed.

Sucked on his lip like a hungry calf, his breath warm and sweet.

She pushed into him. Wrapped around him. Sliding.

Gwen shivered a shudder she shook. She felt his hunger. Hard and deep. Her new body was hungry. For his hunger.

Suddenly it was skin on skin. Wet. Sweet. Warm. His breath on her new breasts, only they didn't seem so strange now, they're wired with heat, right into her wet, in her belly, deep as he sucked on her, licked her moan to the bone. That's me, Gwen found herself thinking, I'm the one moaning.

"Are you sure?" he whispered.

Gwen was sure. Pushed against him, trying to will him inside. She grabbed him hard, the soft hot rock flesh, pulling him in, saying yes.

She didn't know exactly how it happened, but they were incredibly naked.

She grabbed at him with her wet, felt herself climbing waves washing over her, shooting through her heart, growling through her throat, springing from her mouth, out her eyes, into his blue hunger.

"Are you sure?" he whispered.

Gwen felt her wet welling, her new breasts pressed to his chest, his blue, she knew how much he wanted, she wanted. Gwen swallowed him and squeezed him so hard so large and hot filling her she holds him there inside her wet she squeezes shivers shakes, lava flowing through her core to the root to the stem, a melt, giving it to him, taking it from him, letting it go. She made a sound she never heard, a rock-steady pagan rumbling tremble. I want, she said with her eyes, deeper, deepest, and he's trembling, trying to hold back but she's sucking him into her, swimming in his blue. He tries to pull back but she grabs him and wraps her legs around him, grabbing him deep inside her hunger, the soft of his blue, and they shiver shake shudder into each other.

Finally he smiled.

"Goooooooooooooooooooooooall!"

Lunch Meeting

By Marie Sudac

I show up at your office just in time for lunch. I know I shouldn't, but I sneaked a look at your datebook and saw that you don't have anything planned for today at noon. The receptionist is on the phone; she recognizes me and waves me in. Everyone in the offices surrounding you has already slipped out for lunch. I find you in your office on the phone, talking about some contract or something. I close the door, pull the blinds, and look at you.

You register surprise as I pull up my short, businesslike skirt. I'm not wearing any panties, just a pair of thigh-high black stockings with lace tops that hook to my garters. I've shaved for you.

I pull my skirt back down and start toward you.

I come around the side of your desk as you say "Uh-huh, uh-huh. Okay, tell him to add the reversion clause." I'm down on my knees in an instant, and I have your pants open before you can say "Mike, I'll have to call you back. I'm late for a lunch meeting." By the time I hear the phone hit its cradle, I've got your cock in my mouth and it's getting hard quickly. My lips slide up and down on your shaft and I press it back until it touches the back of my throat. You're moaning softly, your hands going through my hair. I suck your cock until you're good and hard, and then I look up at you and see in your fiery eyes how much you want me.

I pull my skirt back up and climb into your lap, facing you. I guide your cock, sticky with my spit, between my lips. As I sink down on you, I'm a little surprised at how wet I am, at how good it feels. I knew I'd be turned on, but I swear I could almost come as I feel the thick head of your cock pressing against the walls of my pussy. I lean forward and kiss you on the lips, my tongue teasing yours as you moan. I start to fuck myself up and down on top of you, unbuttoning my shirt to free my breasts in their tight push-up bra. I pop one breast out of its cup and guide the hard nipple to your mouth; you start to suck it as I continue grinding my hips up and down on top of you, pushing your cock into me.

You lean over, reach out, and draw your arm across your desk, sweeping everything violently to the floor. You pick me up in your arms and push me onto the desk, my ass right at the edge and my legs still spread around you. The desk is the perfect height for you to fuck me, which you do with increasing enthusiasm as you lean forward to suckle both my breasts. Your cock pounds into me and I know I'm going to come soon, but you're not finished with me yet.

You pull out of me, ease me down off the desk, and turn me around. I'm like a doll in your hands as you force me over the edge of the desk, pushing me down against it so I have to spread my legs. Then you enter me from behind, and reach under to press my clit as you start to fuck me.

I have to bite my lip to keep from moaning loudly; it feels so fucking good the way you're working my clit and fucking me that I know I'm going to come any instant. I grab your hand and bite the palm to gag myself, bringing a whimper from your lips as I come in a muffled groan as you pound into me. My muscles clench around your shaft with each thrust, my orgasm overwhelming me as I chew on your hand. Then you're wrenching it from my grasp so you can grasp my hips, holding me in the right position. You start to fuck me hard, fast, ready to bring yourself off. "Please," I whimper. "Come inside me." I feel your thrusts getting faster and faster, and then you're exploding deep inside me, shooting your come into my pussy as I force myself back onto you, meeting your thrusts with my own.

When you're finished, you tug your cock out and I turn around,

pushing you into your chair so I can get down on my knees and lick
you before your cock softens all the way. The taste of your come and
my pussy excites me still more, making my nipples stiffen. They're
still moist from your mouth and they feel cold in the air-conditioned
office air. I lick you clean and tuck your cock back into your pants,
zip you up, buckle your belt. Then I stand up and pull down my
skirt, keeping my thighs pressed tightly together in a largely vain
attempt to keep from leaking on your office carpet.

I lean forward and kiss you once on the lips.

"Hope it was a productive lunch meeting," I whisper.

"Very productive," you say. "We did some excellent work."

"We'll have to schedule them more often," I say.

"I like them unscheduled" is your answer, as you smirk
up at me.

I walk out past the receptionist, feeling the slickness of you oozing out of my pussy. People drift past me, returning from lunch. But
I'm quite sure that their lunch meetings weren't
nearly as productive as ours.

Train Ride

By Sage Vivant

*A*t the Sunnyvale station, Arlen craned his neck to survey the train. "Interesting. Nobody rides this thing on the weekends."

"Hmmm," Carrie responded, distracted by the family on the platform with a gaggle of unruly children. When Arlen's hand cupped her generous breast, she caught her breath but didn't move. She suspected he wouldn't want her to.

"I was reading an article in the *Chronicle* just last week that the construction is forcing people into their cars," he explained, as his fingers located her steadily growing nipple through her blouse. Could the people on the platform see what was going on? she wondered. "I guess we're one of the few who are still trying to keep congestion and pollution to a minimum," he continued. Circling her nipple over and over, he waited while she regulated her arousal. He knew the surprise of his strong will always disconcerted her at first, and he preferred her compliance to be of a more conscious than frightened nature. So he gave her a few moments to think clearly. But no more than a few moments.

"Your breast feels so firm in my hand," he said quietly into her ear as she continued to stare out the window. "When your nipple is this hard, I know that your cunt is wet. Isn't that right?"

"Yes," she whispered, more furtively than she expected. He was right, of course. At his touch, her juices always began to flow and as she sat obediently still in her seat, a tiny stream of wetness spread from her swollen pussy lips to her panties.

"And if I were to caress you between your legs, I would find you wet and ready for me, wouldn't I?" His hand remained on her screaming nipple, rubbing it insistently. If she squirmed, he might be displeased. She remained immobile, stewing in her own juices, only vaguely aware that the train had started moving again.

"Yes," she agreed. "I am wet and ready for you."

They heard movement in the next car as she spoke. Arlen moved his hand from her breast to her crotch, and as he burrowed between her thighs along the seam of her jeans, she spread her legs as much as the seat would allow. "That's a good girl. Give me your wetness. Can you feel the vibration of the train coming up through your cunt?"

She couldn't quite feel it but wanted to. Badly. What she did feel was his tender, expert stroking, applying just enough pressure to make her want to crawl up the back of her seat.

The door of their train car slid open and a conductor walked through. Carrie's eyes widened and her pulse raced as she realized that Arlen had no intention of removing his hand. The conductor stood beside Arlen and asked for their tickets, taking great pains to ignore Arlen's hand busily working at her pubis. As soon as the man moved to the next car, Arlen got up and led Carrie to the bathroom at the front of the car.

She followed anxiously, and when he fingered her dripping pussy in the tiny compartment, she was grateful that the sounds of the train drowned out her shouts of pleasure.

Real Redheads

By Lori Selke

"*A*re you a real redhead?" I asked, pushing my hand under her skirt.

Alyssa giggled and scooted her bottom toward my reaching fingers. She was perched in my lap; my other hand had already undone her bra and was pushing up her green fuzzy sweater. She wore a green plaid skirt and green fishnets, too. I didn't even know they made green fishnets. She wore black combat boots, the genuine article rather than high-fashion Docs, and this only added to her charm.

I was surprised at my own boldness. I had only just met Alyssa a few days before, at the farmer's market. She was buying peaches, three perfect yellow beauties, huge and succulent in her small, white hands, tipped with green nail polish.

It had been the windiest day of the season. Tarps were flapping and pulling at their ropes. Corrugated signs were rolling across the pavement. Alyssa's frizzy rust-colored hair was lashing against her cheek, and her short skirt was swirling up against her thighs. Of course, I didn't know her name yet. But I caught myself watching to see if the wind would catch, lift her skirt above her waist, and give me a glance of her panties. I wondered if they were green, too.

I don't know if they were that day, but tonight they are. Emerald green, silky, and becoming slowly suffused with her sweet nether perfume.

Some people have a thing for redheads; I don't. I have a thing for green fishnets, short skirts, and combat boots. And freckles, cinnamon sprinkled on skin smooth as whipped cream.

She was using one hand to keep her skirt in place, and the other to keep the hair out of her eyes, so I reached into the bins, selected a particularly juicy-looking fruit, and dropped it into her bag. "Your hands were occupied," I said by way of explanation.

She smiled and, after the gust of wind died down, chose another peach and handed it to me. "Oh, I forgot something," she said, and reached into her purse (black) and pulled out a notepad and pen. She scribbled something on the paper and handed it to me. "My name's Alyssa," she said. "Glad to make your acquaintance." On the slip of paper was a phone number.

She paid for her peaches and took off at a brisk pace. "That's my work number," she called over her shoulder. "I'm on my lunch break. But I'm not busy this evening; I get off at six." She waved pertly and was gone.

Busted, I thought, and smiled.

Our courtship wasn't a long one. A couple coffees after work, a dinner date, and now we were on my couch, she was perched in my lap, and my hand was up her skirt.

"So you want to know if I'm a real redhead, do you?" Alyssa asked. "How do you plan on finding out?"

"Well, there's a time-honored and traditional method . . . " I said, and hooked my fingers in the waistband of those silky panties.

She giggled. "And what's that?" she asked, though I knew she knew the answer. She spread her thighs slightly as I tugged her panties toward her knees. All that shifting and wriggling had raised a tent in my pants. I think she enjoyed feeling it snug against her butt. Surely some of that squirming was directed toward a purpose.

Once I got her panties out of the way, I worked my hand back toward her butt. I cupped and squeezed it while we necked for a bit. She had sharp little teeth, and kept nipping at my ear and neck. Not that I minded. I just tweaked her nipples in response; she jumped and giggled, throwing her head back so that I could kiss her neck and down into her cleavage.

Meanwhile, my hand was working its way over her thigh to that sweet cleft between her legs. No need to rush, I thought to myself. We both know where this is going. I kneaded her thigh just above the elastic of her green fishnet stockings, and I even chanced rubbing her stomach, which I love but some girls hate because they think they're fat. If she gasped or sucked her stomach in, I knew to stop. But Alyssa did neither. So I let my hand slide downwards a bit, toward her bush.

Only she didn't have one.

She must have seen the look on my face, because she burst out laughing and slipped off my lap, landing with her legs spread and her butt against the arm of the sofa. I recovered quickly, though, and pounced on top of her, plunging my hand again between her legs, finding her wet and ready—and totally smooth, from the mons all the way down. She was still laughing, but her breath was catching as my hand moved against her warmth.

"You naughty girl — you shave!"

She nodded, stifling her laughter with her hand.

"I guess I'll just have to ask, then."

"I'll never tell!" she crowed, and dissolved into fits of laughter, clamping my hand between her thighs as she fell onto her side and clutched her ribs in mirth.

As long as I had her helpless, I took the opportunity to try and remove some more of the clothes that impeded the both of us— although it was tricky, what with my hand imprisoned underneath her skirt, with no signs of reprieve. In fact, it was impossible, but fun to try. Alyssa wasn't the only one who knew how to use her teeth. And although I couldn't do more than tug at her sweater with them, it did provide me with an excuse to kiss her again. And again. And eventually, her thighs relaxed their grip on my hand, and her fingers found the fly of my pants, and pretty soon I was rubbing my bare hard-on against her bare thigh, and Alyssa was sighing, "Let's wrap that thing up and get down to business."

And not too much later, when I'd sunk deep into her and she was busy stroking her clit frantically, and I could feel her muscles inside grasp and release, grasp and release, she started moaning one word over and over. "Yes," she'd breathe, clasping me around the neck and whispering into my ear. "Yes," she cried as her head thrashed against the sofa cushion. And finally, pounding the upholstery with her clenched fist, "Yes!" And I felt her come, and it wasn't too much longer until I did, too. And when I did, her eyes flew open, and one last time she hollered "Yes!" and then collapsed into giggles again.

I was still panting from the exertion. "Was I that good?" I asked with an ironic smile.

"Yes," she said, grinning and touching my nose. "And yes."

"Yes what?" I said.

"Yes, I am a natural redhead."

It was my turn to fall back into helpless laughter. Alyssa finally had to smother it in kisses. Which was not such a bad outcome after all.

The Long Walk Home

By Darklady

He pushed her out of the car. "Out of the car, bitch," he said as her feet felt gravel beneath them.

Then he drove away.

She stood for a moment at the side of the road, watching his taillights recede and fade. Good riddance to bad garbage, she might have said, squaring her shoulders and beginning her walk towards home. But she didn't. Instead, she looked around to see if anyone was watching. Then she squatted in the middle of nowhere under a bright, full moon, and peed carefully beneath her lifted skirt, missing her sensible shoes and listening as the warm liquid soaked into the spring ground.

At least he'd done it on a nice night this time, she thought, standing, shaking her thighs, and straightening her skirt. Last time it had been pouring rain. She'd been sick for a week with a cough that rattled in her chest enough to catch people's attention. That had been a date to remember.

She felt warmth and wetness on her upper thighs that wasn't urine. She dabbed at it with the skirt, grumbling irritably. It wasn't like it would leave a stain, he'd have told her—and she'd have agreed—but she always winced a bit when she sopped up body fluids with her favorite clothes. Some of them require extra care afterwards. Velvet, for instance. But not cotton-poly blends. Even blood wouldn't ruin them, in small amounts and promptly washed out.

She squared her shoulders and began walking towards home.

She was glad, not for the first time, that she'd found these shoes. On sale, too. They were so comfortable; they even looked good. She could wear them with jeans, slacks, or the long, straight skirts she preferred to wear with her pullover sweaters. Her Bohemian charm expanded her range of wardrobe options. It was one of the things that he loved about her, this eccentric frugality she wore like the shoes she walked in. Simple, elegant, functional, gently irreverent—patient.

It was a good night for a walk. Clear and crisp enough to motivate a walker but not so chill as to discourage one. She could see for miles from the road. It was one of the reasons why they liked to drive there in the first place. Tonight's moon extended the horizon even farther than usual.

She remembered the night they had pulled over, spread a blanket on the trunk of the car and fucked under that enormous moon. She had bled between her legs, it being her time of the month, as she leaned against the back window and watched the heavy round disk—blood red itself—rest briefly upon his bare buttocks as he pumped pleasure into her.

They had lain facing one another, each watching the moon—he as it reflected in the back window, she as it rose between his legs—and whispering their secrets into one another's ears. There had been kisses. On noses. On eyebrows. On lips. On chins. There had been little nibbles. And then more kisses. He had rolled beside her, slipping an arm under her neck and atop her shoulders. They rested and watched the moon move across the sky on its rounds. Then he had kissed her shoulder and audibly whispered into her skin, "The moon says goodbye and so, my dear, must I."

He had rolled her off of the warm blanket and onto the crisp autumnal ground. It was time to go home. It was time for her to walk. It was time for the next move in their game of love.

"See ya later, bitch," he had said, tossing her clothing on the earth near her. "See ya in town."

Then he had driven away; the tang of her skin still on his lips, the spice of her musk still on his fingers, his nostrils.

She had stood for a moment as she always did, watched those twin embers fade from view and shivered—more in her spirit than in her skin. She had felt so warm that she thought she must surely have burned brighter than the bloody moon that had hung heavy behind her. Then she had remembered the gore and cum finger-painting its way down her inner thighs and she had laughed aloud.

Remembering that not dissimilar evening, she laughed again and felt a not dissimilar warmth growing within her. She shivered and hugged herself. She felt loved and special. Today in particular, on this anniversary of sorts. She brushed a lock of brown, wavy hair from in front of her eyes and smiled, lost in her thoughts as she walked.

A second presence advanced, distant but moving closer on the stillness of the road. A driver. Perhaps lovers returning from a tryst under the moon. She moved farther right along the shoulder of the road as a courtesy to the vehicle and a margin of safety for herself.

The car stopped beside and slightly in front of her. The door opened as she glanced toward it.

"Get in, bitch," he said. "You've got something I want and I'm not going to wait all night for you to walk home before I can enjoy it."

She smiled quietly, and moved close to the car. He took her wrist and pulled her beside him. Then they drove away.

Within

By M. Christian

My five fingers, my five cocks, my five dildos, touch and probe and move, knocking to be let in—all the way in. Such a harsh word for such intimacy. Maybe "reaching"? Maybe "handling"—but not "fisting." Too rough, too violent.

The mechanics of it are here, on a table next to the sling or someplace near the bed: wherever the place, they are there. Roll call: gloves (comfortable, surgical if you fancy that), lube (lots and lots and lots and lots—if you think you have enough you don't have enough), and the other things that she might need (vibrator, small whips, dildo, whatever else). These are the keys, necessary but artificial—the facts of life.

The rest, though, is not artificial—way, way beyond artificial.

My gloved hand knocks, wanting in.

Carefully, I dance with her lips, waltz with her minora, majora. She leads, naturally. She takes my hand with her cunt and shows me herself. She opens w-i-d-e, says hello, invites me in. I bow, caress, and take a first step. One finger, with a come hither action. Not a lot. Not a lot at all—just a first step, one finger through the threshold. I hand one finger in her pussy, her cunt, her vagina. One finger inside her, feeling the heat of her, taking her temperature from inside—a special, intimate, inside.

She nods, I nod, and we take another step; both listening to the music she makes.

Two is small. Just two. Two is a little number—just one and one. I move them inside her, feeling around, getting to know this special

place, feeling her interior architecture. I feel a rough spot (G), the nar-
rowing, slick walls (to cervix), the hard jab of bone under, the tight
muscles over, the way her lips move, the way they won't.

Lube and more lube. She shines, glimmers with it, looking red-
mirrored with the slickness, and her own slickness as well.
I note the smile she gives me, with the rise and salute of her clit.
Some women like it touched, during this, some don't. I ask, and she
nods, so I do: bathing her bead with a careful rotation of
my thumb.

Then—three.

Still a small number, a little number. Three isn't a lot, but the tightness has started. The play of one and one and one isn't as flexible as
just one, just two. It's harder to move now, but I have a feel for the
land, for the flow of her lips and walls. I slowly turn my hand, rotating
it slowly, pushing gently, massaging but not forcing her muscles, cooing
with a special kind of sign language to her cunt, pussy, vagina: No one
here who doesn't love you, no one here who means you any harm. Let
me in and we'll dance . . .

Three fingers, bent together: turning slowly, pushing oh-so-gently
at the strength of her cunt. Not forcing. Complying, yes; easing, yes;
massaging, yes; enticing—oh, yes! She opens wider, slowly allowing
me passage in. Her door yields to my three long, reaching fingers.

Inside, within, I tap her G-spot, feeling its corrugated pleasure.
Within, I explore the architecture of her interior.

More lube, some conversation. I ask and she answers: all is well. I
stroke and ring her clit, making her smile wide and magical.

Four. When all you have is five, four is a big number. Actually all
you do have is four—five is the thumb. Four now inside. Four fingers
in a squeezed duckbill, forced so my tips touch together. Four inside,
pushing gently but still firmly, firm but still gentle: Inside her.

Fingers are long and thin, pointed and supple (aside from the small nuts of their joints)—I perform an origami of my own hand: collapsing it, curling my fingers, cupping her from inside, sliding and dancing within her. The hard, literal, part is next, knocking on the door, wanting to be let in.

The hard part is next. I tell her as much.

She breathes, controlling the pain and pleasure that has painted her in reflections of sweat, preparing herself for the reverse birth— taking someone in rather than pushing someone out.

The hard part is the thumb and bones of my hand, the knuckles. I watch her face, hypnotized by her beauty and bravery, amazed by the dance of delight that flickers and swells over her eyes (closed in concentration, open in amazement and near shock), lips (blowing bow kisses, hissing past the pain), and nose (buttoning with the rest of her face). Bathing her clit with my lube-shiny thumb, I ask, polite and civil, if she would be so kind as to allow me into her most inner of sanctums.

Her yes is silent but obvious: with a few gentle turns of the hand, she relaxes and allows me the space and time and delight to push those last few inches in. The hard part is over, the knuckles are through.

Welcome.

This is it: I am inside and filling. This is it, one hand within. The rest is icing on the desert: I have to do is close my long, long (sometimes too long) fingers around my thumb. Fisting ... still too rough and violent. I am inside, within—that says it all.

I watch the pleasure and the pain (more former than latter) dance on her face as I slowly, slowly, slowly turn my hand with a gentle twist, rubbing my knuckles across her G-spot.

Yes, it's my hand, my fingers, my gentle pressure behind it all— but she is in control: she can say "yes", "no", "stop", "slow", "out". I would, of course, because even though it is my hand it is her temple

I am walking slowly into: a supplicant, a respective worshiper: Whatever you say, Goddess.

Then she does say it—after quakes of pounding comes paint her even more with reflective sweat she clenches down on my hand, arches her spine. She says "Out" and I do, telling her to push against my hand, to squeeze me out as I gently withdraw.

Then I am.

I clean up, kissing her hot tummy. I rub her from breasts to legs, from arms to cheeks, from the top of her head to the dimple of her navel. I put a warm blanket over her and hold her while she drifts towards sleep, falls towards exhausted slumber. I follow close behind, having come much deeper from my hand—from being within—than ever from my cock.

Sod

By Greg Wharton

I had to get out of the room. Last night was the viewing, today the funeral. I had been cooped up in the motel room playing dice games with my mother and father for two nights now. I needed some fresh air. Or a drink, or a fuck. A vision of Mike's face popped into my mind, and my cunt trembled, catching me off guard. I'll settle for fresh air, I thought, as I excused myself and left the room feeling more than a little flushed and embarrassed.

We had all come together for the funeral of my grandmother, the family matriarch. Death was about the only thing that ever brought us all together from where we'd scattered through the years. So here I was in Richmond, Indiana, where once upon a time my family all grew up, married, bred, and died.

I had long been gone, and although I kept up with parts of my family, I had lost contact with the rest. I hadn't seen my cousin Jeremy and his wife for 20 years. They were the only ones to stay in Richmond. He and his wife, the same age as me at 37, already had three daughters, a son, and a granddaughter. One daughter married and pregnant with her second child, and the second daughter, Cindy, a senior in high school and already engaged.

Engaged to Mike, easily one of the most beautiful men I had ever met.

A car slowly tailed me down the dark street. Should I be worried in Richmond? Yes, I quickly decided. I was ready to break into a run when it pulled up beside me and I saw Mike's face grinning at me.

"Where you off to?" His smile and his car kept even with my continued walk.

"I needed some fresh air. What are you—"

"Have you ever seen a sod farm?"

"A sod farm? No, Mike, I don't think so." I stopped and gazed into his large clear eyes. A sod farm? Oh, he was so beautiful.

"Hop in, I'll take you. What else you got to do? It's all right, come on!"

Well, I had wanted some fresh air, and it was my last night in Indiana. Why not? I climbed in the car and squirmed as I thought about the other thing I had wished for earlier. Not a drink, that suddenly dropped lower on my list.

The first time I saw him was at the viewing, where relatives and friends are supposed to find closure with death. This family tradition left me feeling depressed and nauseous as relative after relative, stranger after stranger, filed in to stare at Grandma's pale body. We stood around for three hours making small talk, avoiding the subject of my recent divorce. I did my best at playing the good daughter for my parents, spending most of the evening trying not to burst into tears.

I didn't talk to him until towards the end of the evening. Mike, tall, dark, and built like a bull. Solid. Strong. Handsome. Mmmmm. Look at those hands, such nice large hands. Thick fingers, shiny nails. Out of high school, but so young. Shame on me. I couldn't keep my eyes off him. He was magnificent.

I asked the young couple their plans, and tried to sound interested as my cousin's little girl shyly talked on, while I stared into his pretty brown eyes, wishing I were still that young.

It was amazing: the tender young grass was so soft under my bare feet. Mike had insisted I take off my sandals before walking more than two feet into the dark field. The sod was like downy hair. My soles were tickled as I gingerly walked over the moist grass. He grabbed my hand, and my body shivered as I felt his large warm palms. I was instantly wet, and felt the once-familiar itch that I had been ignoring since Charles left me. He tugged my arm, and we ran from one end of the field to the other, then fell panting on our backs as we stared up at the sky rich with stars and a large crescent moon. The moon is never that large or bright in Chicago. I realized how much I missed seeing the stars at night. When was the last time I looked up?

His hands were quick, and had my skirt pulled off before I could object, even if I had wanted to. I didn't have anything on underneath and was ready to come just from the sensation of the baby grass against my bare skin.

His large finger slid in easily and was soon followed by his tongue. Well, he may have looked young, but he had the right technique. The rush hit me. Nothing but his finger inside me, his tongue on my clit, and the grass up my ass. My legs shook. I gripped his hair and cried out. He didn't stop until I had ridden the largest orgasm since, well—since before I even met my now-gone husband.

"Fuck me," I gasped when he came up for air.

"I sure would like to, Michelle, but I can't. I've promised myself, and Cindy, I would stay a virgin until our marriage night."

"A virg—"

"That doesn't mean that we can't have more fun, though!"

He gave me an evil smile as he pulled my shirt off, then gripped each of my nipples between his fingertips, pinching softly as they hardened under his touch.

A virgin? The way he just got me off? Is he for real?

I was truly stuck for words as I watched him stand and quickly strip off his clothes, then climb over me, positioning himself on all fours with his mouth at my cunt and his cock aimed down at my face. He slipped his finger back into me and his cock into my mouth.

His cock was fat, no, more like muscular. Like him. Large, solid muscle. I pulled it out of my mouth and gripped it with both hands, wondering if he and his soon-to-be wife did this. I stuck my tongue out and licked its head. While he continued to finger my cunt, his lips and tongue explored my clit. I opened wide and started pumping my mouth around his cock, trying to keep time with him.

My second orgasm was building, and he hadn't tired of my cunt yet. Lucky Cindy! His body was straddling me now, and though numb, my face and mouth had become accustomed to his cock's deep thrusts. The skin on his cock was so smooth, and I could feel the huge veins that ran up his length rubbing against my lips and tongue as he forced in and out. His balls bounced roughly against my nose and forehead as I felt the welcome new sensation of a finger worming into my asshole.

I screamed out again as the field shook under me, but was muffled by the thick cock in my throat. I did the only thing I could think of; I licked, then worked my finger into his asshole too. His whole body twitched and he shot into my throat, not missing a thrust. When he was done I rolled him off, so he was kneeling beside me. I licked my finger again and slid it back into his ass, then harder, and licked at his cock as he watched me in wonder. I felt like worshiping it, like he had me. I wiggled my finger back and forth, and lapped at the veins still bulging out the length of him.

The force of his ejaculation actually made me think that maybe I really was the first. No, I couldn't be. He hadn't said that. He just meant he hadn't fucked. Oh, how I wanted him to fuck me.

"Are you really a virgin?" I asked between slurps up his length.

He grinned at me, but didn't answer. Instead he rocked hard against my fingers probing his ass, and surprisingly, within minutes rewarded me with another mouthful of his come as he howled out like a wolf at the moon.

We lolled together in the field for a long time and watched the stars without speaking. I felt such peace for a change and wanted to just curl up beside him and sleep, but we both knew that we should go. We dressed slowly, watching the last of each other's grass-stained bodies disappear, then walked silently back to his car. I took one last look at the sky, and closed my eyes, making sure to remember each star.

My sleep was deep my last night in Richmond. I left for an early flight back home feeling more rested, better, than I had in years, and yet still sad.

As I watched my parents wave at me from the airport window, I felt overwhelmed by bittersweet emotions. My grandma was gone, and I was leaving my family. How many years until the next time we would be pulled together by death? How many years will pass before I see parts of my family again?

And Mike. I could still smell him. When would I see him again? Would I see him again?

I couldn't decide which would bother me more, hearing news that Mike and my cousin's little girl got married, or that they didn't. Either way, I would never forget the sensation of baby grass on my bare skin.

Spank Me

BY RACHEL KRAMER BUSSEL

"Spank me." The words hovered at the edge of my mind, ready to burst forth in release, but I held them back for a few more moments. They'd waited there long enough. I was still nervous, even though I'd been mouthing them, thinking them, fantasizing them, wanting to say them, for two months, but so far had let them remain a part of my dream world rather than my actual life. What would happen after I said them, after I asked my boyfriend, Darren, to fulfill this most treasured of fantasies? Would he laugh? Would he be excited? Aroused? Horrified? Angry? Confused? I had no idea what his reaction might be. We'd been dating and sleeping together for a little over a year, and our relationship and sex life were happy, pleasant, fun. There was nothing to really complain about, but I was looking for something more. Something very specific.

For the past few weeks, our fun but routine sex life somehow hadn't been enough. We'd both come in the same predictable ways (me on top or alternating oral sex), then I'd lay awake while Darren slept, dreaming of being sprawled across his lap, one of my flimsy skirts hiked up over my hips, my panties pulled tightly between my cheeks, and his hands slapping me, making me squirm, making me hot. It was all I could do not to bring his hands up to my cheeks, to try to communicate my desires telepathically, but something stopped me. We'd never talked about spanking or anything kinky in the past, so perhaps it was foolish of me to think he'd be able to intuit what I wanted. But foolish or not, I wanted him just to turn me over and bring his hand down hard on my ass, and keep on doing it until he was ready to stop. I tossed and turned, wiggling, dreaming of my butt on fire, red with heat and passion.

Darren finally awoke, and could tell that I was in a bit of an agitated state. He reached around and tweaked my nipples while he licked the back of my neck and sighed into my skin. This felt heavenly, but right then I was looking for a little bit of hell. I pushed my ass back against him, feeling his hard hot cock against my cheeks. I reached around and brought his hand from my breast downwards, placing it on my ass and moving it back and forth. I turned around and kissed him deeply, my own hand
sliding down to his ass and giving a squeeze. "Darren, there's something that you can do that would make me so happy. I've been lying here for the last hour thinking about it and it's making me so wet and so excited." Then I looked him in the eye and said, "I want you to spank me." I wasn't simpering, or overly breathy, but I wasn't quite as bold as I'd have liked to be. I sucked in my breath as soon as the words were out, worried that I'd made a mistake by entrusting my most treasured fantasy to my most treasured person. My heart felt like it was about to beat right out of my chest. I could feel it thudding and pounding with the kind of nerves I usually only get at the office, but now I was feeling that way in front of my boyfriend, my lover whom I could trust with anything. At least, I hoped I could trust him with this.

He stared at me for a minute, and started to open his mouth like he was going to speak, but then he didn't. He turned me over so I was lying across his lap, and I could feel his cock poking against me, hard and firm and eager. I did what I usually do in that situation, sliding back and forth against him, trying to provoke him. But it didn't have the usual reaction. He pulled my hair so that my head lifted and I was staring right at him. "None of that for now, I'll tell you when I'm ready." The fierce tone of his voice sent shivers running throughout my body. I put my head back down, nervous and excited at once, a small smile peeking out despite my resolve to be stoic and calm. Then his hand came crashing down on my ass. It was nothing, and everything, like I'd dreamed about. It tingled and hurt for a moment, like I'd expected, but then I started to feel warm all over, craving more of the same rough treatment. I felt a shot of desire run through my cunt, leaving me feeling like I truly had a desperate hole to fill. Then he did it again and I felt my whole body go liquid, relaxed, melting. I let out the tiniest of moans and twisted, squirming with the thrill of his smacks.

I could tell from the way he grunted as he did it that he was both annoyed and turned on. He doesn't usually like it when I decide that things are going to change; he likes some time to ease into any new developments. I know that, but there was no way for me to tell him gradually; this was an all or nothing deal. From then on, I let my body do the talking. And I guess it was getting my message across pretty well, because I felt his hand continue to spank me, again and again, working up a rhythm as he went faster and faster, each blow blurring into the last and the next. I could feel a new kind of heat rising from my skin. It hurt, but mostly it felt hot, a delicious, addictive heat, and I kept wanting more. I twisted my head around to get a peek, and saw his hand come slamming down into my skin, over and over like a racquet hitting a ball swiftly and precisely, knowing exactly where to strike. I turned back around and shut my eyes, afraid of what I might do with the sensations that had just swept through my body as I watched him. The more he spanked me, the more I wanted him to. I glimpsed another peek, this time at his face, furrowed in concentration. His cock was still pressing against me, hard as could be. I wriggled against it happily, glad I'd finally gotten the words right.

Honeymoon

By David Henry Sterry

Two. In Jennifer. The image made her melt into wet.

It was their honeymoon, and Jennifer and William were laying totally naked in Kauai, the Garden Island, the sun melting their bones, smell of coconut oil baking on their hot skin, seasalty air floating on the thick breeze, the overgrown tropical paradise intoxicating.

William smiled at Jennifer. Yes, people may be starving, the whole world may be crumbling, but at least this one thing worked out.

Jennifer quarter-dozed and half-floated.

Honeymooning.

Jennifer loved how his eyes were so wild and kind. How his hand moved over her body. How his hair was different every day. She saw herself growing old with him.

William loved the way her laugh tasted. How her smell made his stomach jump. He saw himself a year from now kissing her big pregnant belly.

Jennifer sucked on big finger, and felt her socket plugged in, juice jolting through her, the wet heat flooding her gates, the thick of William getting thicker.

Jennifer had never had an orgasm before William. But now, on their honey, moony beach, her orgasm peeked easily through a crack in her wall and waved.

William pulled her on top, and she slid up him easy as you please, one knee on either side of his head, looking down into his wild kind eyes, her sex inches from his breath and she smelled like perfect love.

Jennifer lowered herself so his tongue tip grazed her sex lip, and he licked her slow, like a love-flavored ice cream cone.

Jennifer watched William, his thickness in hand, so familiar, yet always a revelation, the slapslapslapping of flesh, a tiny droplet glistened in the sun.

William sucked her swollen and hard, just the way she liked it.

Jennifer slipped back down him, grabbed him, wide-open and wanting. At the tip of her he stopped.

"No baby, put it in," she whispered. She tried to slide him into her, but he held her tight.

"Are you sure?" he asked.

"Oh yes, please," she said, never more sure of anything.

"What do you want?" he asked, keeping the tip of his thickness at the tip of the very wet Jennifer.

"I want you inside of me, please," she moaned.

He put a thick inch into her. "Is that enough?"

She tried to suck more into her, but he held her strong.

"No, baby, I want all of it, pleeeease." She was almost screaming now with the need and the tease, so close, but held tight, immovable.

"This is all for you," he grabbed her hips and she arched herself wide open, so William could go all the way inside Jennifer, where she had never wanted anyone.

Jennifer felt like she was gonna black out from all that William.

He felt the soul of the Garden Island flow through them.

Suddenly, magically, there he was: the man. Big deep round face. Long hair, wavy black, pushed back from his forehead. Big deep brown smiling eyes. Muscles smooth a glistening of sun and ocean. Naked. Standing over them.

Jennifer and William looked at each other. Then they looked back at him. He was still there. Smiling a deep sweet smile. Before they even knew it, they were smiling back at him.

He took himself largely in hand and put himself next to Jennifer's lips. Just put it there. Next to her lips.

She took the tip of him, soft little kisses, hip muscles undulating on William, and she sucked a little more of the man in her mouth.

Jennifer had never felt so full in her life.

The man was now fully thickened, blazing glazing ecstasy throwing head back, arms open, sun bathing face:

"Ahhhhhhhhhhh!"

Jennifer's cum was right there, in extreme close-up, as she rocked on William, sucking on the man, throat opening as tremors trembled her.

Then Jennifer did something completely unexpected. She took the man in hand, brought him down to his knees, and put the tip of him on William's lips and kissed them, licking, little nibbles, her husband's mouth and the man's thickness at the same time.

Then William did something that he never thought he would do. He opened his lips and sucked on the tip of that man, all hot and hard and big.

She rocked and shook at the sight of all this, and her cum finally won:

"Oh-h-h-h-h-h-h-h-h-h-h my-y-y-y-y-y-y-y-y-y-y-y-y-y Go-o-o-o-o-o-o-o-o-o-o-o-d!"

When Jennifer parachuted back down she guided the man behind her, and he ran his hand across Jennifer's beautiful back, salty sweaty slick with sun and desire. He spread her apart a little and he pressed that largeness against the tip of her behind, so hard and so still as she moved William in and out of her. Jennifer growled again, the craving raising Cain in her, wailing to be full.

Jennifer looked into William and asked with her eyes if it was all right. He smiled back that it was. The man lathered himself up with coconut oil. While he teased the tip of her she pulled up and down on William and groaned each time, another cum rushing forward.

As Jennifer thought—*there is no way all that is gonna fit*—she spread herself, feeling the man throbbing in her sweet, and she pushed back so slow the coconut oil so slippery, and just the head of his thick slid into her.

The suddenness of it was almost too much, a sweet ache shivering through the big heat beating inside her.

Jennifer deep-breathed, and clenched her tingling, the skin so thin between her husband's thickness and the throb of the knob of the man. She had never in her sweet short life felt so full of so much, so tight, the pressure swollen so full.

Jennifer pushed back on the man and then he was all the way in. Almost too full. Almost. She breathed and squeezed both of them now, and she shook and she felt it coming round the mountain riding six white horses, as William buried himself in her.

"O God," growled out of Jennifer. "O Jesus," growled out of William.

Then William was gushing buckets of rainbows, colors everywhere, and the man spasmed hot, and shot tropical. And that made Jennifer flower, as she was swept away again, and they all leapt off together, beyond her and him, swandiving, Icarus soaring, ballistic, sirens singing, and the walls cum a-tumblin' down.

The man, drugged with the love of Jennifer and William, threw his head back and arms open, exhaled a sun-bathed:

"Ahhhhhhhhhhh!"

The ocean roared in applause and the trees danced and sang.

Jennifer collapsed into William and they melted into each other, into the warm white sand slipping into a tropical sleep of deep paradise.

When they woke up the pink sun was winking goodbye.

The man was gone. They were alone.

Jennifer and William smiled into each other's eyes, lighted by the honey dripping off the moon.

The Magician's Assistant

By Cecilia Tan

The magician's assistant is looking at herself in the mirror, trying to attach a sequin to just the right spot on her face. The makeup mirror shows the tiny wrinkles beginning to appear as she squints and turns her head from side to side, the white Vegas feather plume wig rustling against her bare shoulders as she looks at the curve of her cheeks, the dimple of her chin. The damn sparkle needs to be placed just so or it'll look like a crystalline cancer on her face instead of a little bit of magic. The plastic gem poised on her index finger, a tiny dab of spirit gum glistening, she points her hand at her reflection, reflecting. He was going to put her in chains tonight, and then plunge her into a glass-sided tank filled with cold water, and then a bunch of other mumbo jumbo, the result of which always was she emerged elsewhere miraculously freed, but also soaked to the bone in her see-through dress, nipples erect … it's Vegas, after all.

She waves the sequin in the mirror and thinks … hmm. She pulls the clingy white fabric away from her breast and plants the sequin onto her nipple. She gets another from the tray on her makeup table and makes the other nipple to match. She poises a third, but hesitates. This magician isn't really much fun. He's married and is putting two kids through college and she doesn't really see very much of him beyond a few lame rehearsals and the show itself. She's had bosses before who appreciated the situation a bit more, shall we say. Who could find the rabbit under her dress. Who sawed her in half after hours.

What the hell, she thinks, so he'll never know. She hikes up the glittering Elizabeth-Taylor-as-Cleopatra dress and slides down in the chair. Her knees fall open and her hand hovers under the makeup table. Her face is ringed by soft white bulbs all the way around as her unseen finger places the last jewel in one place no one is likely to see it tonight. She presses it into place and gasps, transfixed by her own reflection, at the half-lidded look of longing on her face. Maybe tonight the dress will tear in the water, under the chains. Maybe tonight she will shine.

The Suit

By Steven Schwartz

Watching her husband turn around in front of the mirror, she thought to herself that she'd forgotten how good he could look. She was embarrassed to admit it, but it was true. Until someone else went to great lengths to show him at his best, she couldn't always see past the everyday of shirt-and-jeans. He looked fine, now.

Some of it, beyond the faintest shadow of a doubt, was the woolen fabric. It was dark and smooth, and hung just right. It emphasized his wrists where they emerged from the sleeves, the back of his neck standing out against the white shirt and dark collar. It didn't hide him so much as wrap him, smoothing out the rough edges and imperfections. The scar from where he'd needed the pin put in his shoulder, after he fell from the roof? She couldn't see it now, and he moved as if it wasn't there, when the tailor asked him to lift his arms, so he could check the jacket's fit.

Adjusting the fit here and there, the tailor moved around him, marking places that needed to be altered with a stub of white chalk. She suddenly wished she'd learned about tailoring, so that it could be her hands there, instead. She would not have to be so professional while measuring his inseam, for example. How was he reacting to having another man touch him there, she idly wondered. He was probably used to it by now. He'd had suits fitted before. If she were measuring him, that inseam measurement would change, as her fingers stroked him through the thin, soft fabric.

Perhaps, she thought as she sat back in her chair, it was best she wasn't the tailor. They'd never get the fitting over with. She returned to the question of what made the suit so attractive.

It wasn't just that he looked thinner. She didn't mind him a little round about the middle; it made him more comfortable to lean against in bed, before they started to make love, or when they basked in each other afterwards. And the fact that she enjoyed his padding helped her to enjoy hers. So it was not that he looked thinner, though he'd mentioned several times that you look ten pounds lighter in a good suit. Those missing ten pounds did not make him sexier.

He was cared for, that was it. And it showed. He'd never be willing to let her bathe him, shampoo him and style his hair, but she wanted to. No, he wouldn't be able to keep his hands off her in the shower, or while she worked on his hair. Not that she'd mind it if she was interrupted and swept off to bed, but that was not what she wanted.

But the suit made him look as good as she thought he could. And that made her like it. And made her excited by it. While the tailor walked about with pins held between his lips, adjusting hems, she let her thoughts drift off.

How did she want to have him? It was a difficult choice. He looked so right in The Suit (for it had already acquired capital letters in her mind) that she didn't want him to take it off. But she wanted him, and the suit was in the way. It felt nice, the smooth fabric under her fingers, but she was afraid to touch it too hard, to mar it, to bunch it up as she pulled him close. She didn't want sweat stains under the armpits, or stains from her juices on the suit, from rubbing her thighs against his.

In the end, she knew she'd compromise, and she knew just how. She could be naked, and touch herself, and keep all of her juices on her own hand. All he needed to do—or to let her do—was to undo that fly. There was something very right, and very sexy, about undoing all those secret little flaps on a pair of men's trousers. From the front, they were supposed to look simple—a little seam you would hardly notice. But to get inside, first you had to undo the belt. And the outside button, hidden under the belt. And the zipper, pushing more fabric aside, and then the inside button you'd never know existed from just looking, a last secret little test. Every time she'd heard a man whine about undoing bra straps, she'd think of the pleasures of unwrapping Christmas presents—and this was the same thing.

Once that last button was undone, she could go to work on his underwear—whether it was just reaching in and slipping him out of his boxers, or having a whole new row of buttons to undo, slowly, teasingly. By now he'd be straining to get out, perhaps the head of his cock poking out as she undid buttons. She'd kiss it, just once, and look up at him, look up the length of that white shirt, that dark suit to his face. Maybe she'd want him wearing gloves, so that the only skin of his she could see was his face, and his cock.

Then she would start to suck him off, but her way. One hand down between her legs, the other rubbing against his thigh, against that soft fabric, warm to the touch from his heat. And her eyes would be open, to enjoy the sight of him, looking the best he could. His eyes might be closed, enjoying the warmth of her mouth wrapped around him, but this wasn't about him looking at her. And as her hand brought her closer and closer to orgasm, her fingers finding all her sensitive places, she'd keep her eyes open, no matter how much she wanted to close them and let herself go.

Once she had come, then the suit could come off—and they could do whatever they wanted. And she kept thinking about what that might be, as the tailor kept at his work.

She'd never had this much fun shopping with him before.

Notes on Contributors

Blake C. Aarens is a survivor of childhood sexual abuse who writes award-winning erotica. Her fiction has appeared in the journals *Good News*, *Aché* and *Open Wide*, the anthologies *Herotica 2, 3, 5, Switch Hitters, Sex Spoken Here, Virgin Territory, The Best American Erotica 1993*, and in *Penthouse* magazine. She is currently seeking a publisher for her erotica collection *Gifts of Sex*.

Charlie Anders can never take naps without becoming groggy, but likes the idea of discos with divans. She's the co-publisher of *Other* magazine, the magazine for people who defy categories. Her writings have appeared in *ZYZZYVA*, *Strange Horizons*, *Best Bisexual Erotica 1* and *2*, *Comet*, *Best Transgender Erotica*, and many other magazines and anthologies. Her book *The Lazy Crossdresser* came out in 2002 from Greenery Press. See www.charlie-girl.com.

Lisa Archer has been published (occasionally under a different last name) in *Best Bisexual Women's Erotica*, *Best Fetish Erotica*, *Best Woman's Erotica 2002*, *Mammoth Book of Best New Erotica*, Volume 2, *Best of the Best Meat Erotica* and *Pills, Thrills, Chills, and Heartache*. She has also written for publications such as Agence France-Press (AFP.com), *Adult Industry News* (AINews.com), *Horny? San Francisco*, *Playgirl* magazine, and the *San Francisco Bay Guardian*.

Edward L. Beggs is a former Congregational minister who discovered he had to leave the church to become a whole human being. He was Founder and Director of the nation's first teenage runaway center in San Francisco in 1967 and has published two books with Ballantine Books: *Huckleberry's For Runaways* and *Open House: A Successful New Community Treatment Approach for Young Suburban Addicts*. His non-fiction book: *Skateland: Fifteen California Stories* is forthcoming from Self Reliance Press. He is currently at work on a docu-novel: *Kicking the God Habit*. "Speaking in Tongues" is his first published piece of erotica.

Rachel Kramer Bussel is the reviser of *The Lesbian Sex Book*, co-author of *The Erotic Writer's Market Guide*, and editor of the sex guidebook *Horny? New York*. Her writing has been published in *Bust*, Cleansheets.com, *Curve*, *Diva*, *Girlfriends*, *Playgirl*, *On Our Backs*, Oxygen.com, the *San Francisco Chronicle* and over a dozen erotic anthologies. Find out more at www.rachelkramerbussel.com.

M. Christian's work can be seen in *Best American Erotica, Best Gay Erotica, Best Lesbian Erotica, Best Transgendered Erotica, Best Bondage Erotica, Friction,* and over 150 other anthologies, magazines, and web sites. He's the editor of over 12 anthologies, including *Best S/M Erotica, Love Under Foot* (with Greg Wharton), *Underground* (with Paul Willis), *The Burning Pen, Guilty Pleasures,* and many others. He's the author of three collections, the Lambda-nominated *Dirty Words* (gay erotica), *Speaking Parts* (lesbian erotica), and *The Bachelor Machine* (science fiction erotica). For more information, check out www.mchristian.com.

Greta Christina has been writing about sex since dinosaurs ruled the earth. Her work has appeared in *Ms.*, *Penthouse*, and *On Our Backs* magazines, as well as the *Best American Erotica 2003* collection, an assortment she finds highly amusing. Greta lives in San Francisco.

Kelly Da Crioch is a lifelong Bay Area resident who has written erotica, science fiction, poetry, criticism, and political essays. "Gold" is his first professionally published prose piece.

Darklady is a full-time sex writer, educator, activist, event coordinator, politician, and basically eclectic dark-haired Bohemian chick residing in Portland, Oregon. Her work covers topics as far-ranging as adult video, DVD, book, and toy reviews, responsible non-monogamy, BDSM, erotica, the adult Internet, and free speech. She is a regular reviewer for *Adult Video News* magazine, a lifestyle columnist for *Playtime* magazine, and the Q&A sexpert for the Venus Book Club. Previously published works of erotic fiction are included in the Black Books' anthologies *Best Bisexual Erotica 2*, *Guilty Pleasures*, and *Best S/M Erotica*. You can learn more about Darklady and her plan for a far groovier and more sexually satisfied free world by visiting www.darklady.com.

Marlo Gayle is a naughty jock who enjoys full contact and getting the knots worked out.

Kecia is a Warrior Goddess who lives, works, and plays in San Francisco. She loves reading and writing erotica. "Birthday Rap" is her first published story.

Marilyn Jaye Lewis's erotic short stories and novellas have been widely anthologized in the U.S. and Europe. She is the founder and executive director of the Erotic Authors Association, the first American organization to honor literary excellence in the erotic genre. *When Hearts Collide: An Erotic Romance* will be published in 2003 by Magic Carpet, and *Night on Twelfth Street: Bisexual Erotic Fiction* will be published in 2004 by Alyson Books.

Elise Matthesen lives in Minnesota, surrounded by beads, metal, words, music, friends, lovers, and partners. She has a hearing impairment, fibromyalgia, arthritis, attitude, ingenuity, numerous publication credits, and more than two dozen pairs of pliers.

This is **Robert Morgan**'s first published erotica (although he has been practicing for this moment all his life as an accomplished and inspiring erotic talker). Robert is a sex educator and pleasure activist who lives, teaches, and writes with Carol Queen. They are working on a book.

Muzelle is the fetching nom de plume for Kelly Bodden, who lives in San Francisco and works for Xandria.com. She is a pleasure-driven sensualist learning to embrace unblushingly her fiery libido via erotic writings and other salacious acts. Currently pursuing her Ph.D. in sexology, her ambition is to spread sexual enlightenment across the states via easily accessible sex education and massive exposure . . . even in cow towns.

Carol Queen has a doctorate in sexology. She is an award-winning erotic author and essayist; her novel *The Leather Daddy and the Femme* won a Firecracker Alternative Book Award for Best Sex Book in 1999. She is also the author of *Exhibitionism for the Shy and Real Live Nude Girl*, and she has edited or co-edited six anthologies. See her complete bibliography at www.carolqueen.com. She lives in San Francisco and is a worker/owner at Good Vibrations.

The author of more than 50 books under various names, **Thomas Roche** is also the editor of the *Noirotica* series and has written more than 200 published short stories and 250 published nonfiction articles for web sites, magazines, and anthologies. His most recent books are *His* and *Hers*, two books of erotica cowritten with Alison Tyler.

Lori Selke is the editor of the anthologies *Tough Girls* and *Literotica*. Her stories have appeared in *Best Bisexual Erotica 1* and *Best Bisexual Erotica 2* and in *Zaftig: Well Rounded Erotica*. Sometimes she writes things that aren't about sex, too. She lives in San Francisco. Visit her at http://www.io.com/~selk.

Steven Schwartz wears suits only to the opera and job interviews. His erotic fiction appears in *Best Bisexual Erotica 2*, *Tough Guys*, and *Wired Hard 2*, along with the chapbook *69*, consisting of 69 69-word stories set at a sex party.

Marcy Sheiner is editor of the *Best Women's Erotica* series (Cleis Press) as well as of *Herotica* volumes 4 through 6 (Down There Press and Plume). She is author of *Sex for the Clueless: How to Have a More Erotic and Exciting Life*, and *Perfectly Normal: A*

Mother's Memoir. Having reached the age of wisdom, she sums up what she's learned in one short phrase: Wear black and eat salad. You can visit her at http://marcysheiner.tripod.com/

David Henry Sterry is both author of and performer in "Chicken: A 1-Ho Show," based on his *San Francisco Chronicle* best-seller *Chicken: Self-Portrait of a Young Man for Rent* (ReganBooks, Harper Collins, 2002). The book is being optioned to be made into a film. He is also the author of *Satchel Sez: The Wit Wisdom & World of Leroy Satchel Paige* (Crown, Random House, 2001). He has worked as a stand-up comedian, an actor, and the emcee at Chippendale's Male Strip Club in New York, winning Cabaret Performer of the Year. He has written plays and screenplays. He has worked as a chicken, a chicken frier, soda jerk, a cherry picker, a poet, a building inspector, a barker, and a marriage counselor. He recently completed a twenty-city tour with Chicken. He now volunteers with the Larkin St. Youth Project, doing outreach with homeless kids on the streets of San Francisco. In December, 2002, he was the closing speaker at the Protecting Our Children Summit in Washington, D.C., where representatives from the State Department, the Justice Department, judges, care-providers, law enforcement officials, academics, and survivors met to try and end the commercial sexual exploitation of children.

Marie Sudac is a dancer, poet, and erotica writer who lives in the Los Angeles area with her lover and two cats. Her work has appeared in the anthologies *Sweet Life* and *Slave.*

Cecilia Tan is the author of various books of erotica, including *The Velderet, Black Feathers,* and *Telepaths Don't Need Safewords.*

Her stories have appeared in *Penthouse, Ms., Asimov's Science Fiction, Best American Erotica*, Nerve.com, and elsewhere. She writes about all her passions (sex, food, and baseball) from the Boston area. "The Magician's Assistant" is from the work-in-progress *The Book of Want* and was written for Penn Gillette. More juicy tidbits can be learned at www.ceciliatan.com.

Sage Vivant is the proprietress of Custom Erotica Source http://www.customeroticasource.com, where she and a small cadre of writers have been creating tailor-made erotic fiction for individual clients since 1998. She has been a guest on numerous television and radio shows nationwide. Her work has appeared on various web sites, and been published in *Maxim, Forum UK*, and *Erotica* magazines. Several of her short stories are scheduled to appear in upcoming anthologies.

Melanie Votaw is the author of *52 Weeks of Passionate Sex, Hummingbirds: Jewels on Air, The Art of Chinese Calligraphy*, and *The Cocktail Kit*. Also an extensively published poet and nature photographer, Melanie displays galleries of her work taken on four continents at www.VotawPhotography.com.

Greg Wharton is the publisher of Suspect Thoughts Press and an editor of two web magazines, SuspectThoughts.com and VelvetMafia.com. He is the editor of the anthologies *The Best of the Best Meat Erotica, Law of Desire* (with Ian Philips), *The Love That Dare Not Speak Its Name, Love Under Foot* (with M. Christian), and *Of the Flesh*. A collection of Wharton's short fiction, *Johnny Was and Other Tall Tales*, will be released in 2003. He lives in San Francisco where he is hard at work on a novel.

Yohannon was raised as a proper Irish Catholic boy in New York City, so it was inevitable he would become a polyamorous bisexual pagan switch (with a strong preference for fat people) living in the Santa Cruz mountains. It is suspected that he keeps a special portrait in his attic to avoid looking his age of 40, though he freely admits to feeling that old after a long night of healthy debauchery.